"It's a vanilla milk shake."

"You made me a milk shake?" She couldn't keep the surprise from her voice as she reached out to take it from him, careful not to let their fingers touch in the exchange.

He cocked his head to one side and smiled that toe-curling grin. "Well, you said you didn't want coffee. I couldn't find the ingredients for hot chocolate and you don't like tea, but of course you had ice cream."

"You remembered I don't like tea?" The surprises just kept coming.

He nodded, his gaze trained on hers. "Of course. We're friends, aren't we? Friends remember each other's likes and dislikes."

She swallowed. Friends? Was that what they were? Friends with benefits? Friends who accidentally made a mistake and slept together? Friends who just happened to have conceived a baby?

THE McKINNELS OF JEWELL ROCK:
There's no formula for finding true love!

Dear Reader,

I'm delighted to be sharing with you the second book in my McKinnels of Jewell Rock series. If you read the first book (*A Dog and a Diamond*) you'll have met the McKinnels and their family business, a whiskey distillery in Central Oregon, and you'll have met the hero and heroine of this book.

Pregnant by Mr. Wrong was both fun and challenging to write. Fun because the hero is a secret advice columnist for the town's local newspaper, and challenging because the heroine used to be engaged to his older brother. These two had a brief liaison, but due to their family circumstances and preconceived opinions of each other, they believed it was just a fling.

When Bailey Sawyer finds herself pregnant by Quinn McKinnel, she is confused and has no idea what to do, so she consults the local advice columnist. Unbeknownst to her and everyone they know, Quinn is actually this columnist. In this way, *Pregnant by Mr. Wrong* is my twist on the old favorite, the secret pregnancy storyline—the hero knows about the baby but the heroine does not know he knows. I hope you'll enjoy reading it as much as I enjoyed writing it.

I love hearing from readers via Twitter, Facebook or my website, www.rachaeljohns.com, so please let me know what you think of Jewell Rock and my McKinnels.

Happy reading,

Rachael

Pregnant by Mr. Wrong

Rachael Johns

 HARLEQUIN® SPECIAL EDITION®

Recycling programs
for this product may
not exist in your area.

ISBN-13: 978-0-373-62336-5

Pregnant by Mr. Wrong

Printed in U.S.A.

Rachael Johns is an English teacher by trade, a mom 24/7, a chronic arachnophobe and a writer the rest of the time. She rarely sleeps and never irons. A lover of romance and women's fiction, Rachael loves nothing more than sitting in bed with her laptop and electric blanket and imagining her own stories. Rachael has finaled in a number of competitions, including the Australian Romance Readers Awards—*Jilted*, her first rural romance, won Favourite Contemporary Romance in 2012. She was voted in the top ten of Booktopia's Australia's Favourite Author poll in 2013. Rachael lives in the West Australian hills with her hyperactive husband, three mostly gorgeous heroes in training, two fat cats, a cantankerous bird and a very badly behaved dog. Rachael loves to hear from readers and can be contacted via her website, www.rachaeljohns.com. She is also on Facebook and Twitter.

Books by Rachael Johns

Harlerquin Special Edition

A Dog and a Diamond

HQN

Jilted
The Kissing Season

Carina Press

Stand-In Star
One Perfect Night

To Scarlet Wilson, Helen Lacey,
Fiona Lowe, Melissa James and Leah Ashton
for holding my hand as I wrote this book!
Love you all for all your various help.

Prologue

As Bailey Sawyer stepped into the warehouse at Mc-Kinnel's Distillery, goose bumps painted her arms and her stomach twisted as if doing some elaborate macramé. She glanced around the quiet space, looking and listening for signs of Quinn.

This had always been her favorite part of the distillery. Its walls were lined with new American oak barrels, stacked up one on top of another, almost up to the high ceiling, and there were rows upon rows of barrels down the middle as well, all printed with the famous McKinnel's logo on the end. The thick wooden floorboards almost matched the color of the barrels and the scent of whiskey at various stages of the aging process blended together in the air.

She inhaled deeply, experiencing a heady rush as memories of this place washed over her. She'd been coming to the distillery for as long as she could remember. McKinnel's Distillery, a local institution, had become famous for creating one of America's best boutique whiskeys long before boutique distilleries, breweries and wineries were all the rage. As a child and teenager, she'd hung out here because her mother was best friends with Nora McKinnel. Bailey and the seven McKinnel kids had spent many a day running rampant through the warehouse, chasing each other, playing hide-and-go-seek, making mischief and memories. It had been better than a playground.

For the past five years, she'd been a regular guest due to the fact she'd been dating and then (briefly) engaged to Nora's oldest son, Callum. Their moms had been ecstatic about the union, then dumbfounded and devastated when Bailey had ended it a couple of weeks ago.

But they didn't know the half of it.

The macramé in her stomach tightened as she stepped farther into the building, her knee-high boots echoing as they struck the floor. Today, the familiar scent and the innocent childhood memories didn't calm her. Instead, guilt warred with desire as she called out "Quinn" (before she lost her nerve) and remembered the last time she was in here with him. Although it was late November, the day after Thanksgiving, and the air in here was even cooler than the temperature outside, her whole body, from her fingernails right down to her tippy-toes, heated at the recollection.

She hadn't been cold that night a few weeks ago, either. Quinn's hot bare skin against her own had provided more warmth than an electric blanket, and however wrong it may be, she hadn't been able to get him out of her head since.

"What are *you* doing here?" Quinn stepped out from behind a row of barrels, jolting her thoughts and almost scaring her half to death.

Her heart quivered at his less than enthusiastic greeting, but her hormones jumped up and down in excitement at being so close to him again. He wore only jeans ripped at the knees and a black T-shirt, indicating he'd been doing some physical labor before her arrival. She licked her lips, garnering the courage to speak, the wisdom to know what exactly to say, and tried not to stare at the way his lovely arm muscles peeked out from the sleeves of his T-shirt. He was ripped—that was for sure.

"I thought we should talk about, you know, what happened…" She didn't need to finish her sentence. It didn't take a genius to work out what she was referring to.

Quinn let out an irritated sigh and ran a hand through his thick dirty-blond hair. Despite his obvious annoyance at her presence, Bailey's fingers twitched as she remembered how it had felt when she'd knotted her hands at the back of his head while he'd thrust into her. Her cheeks flamed.

"What's there to talk about?" he asked.

"Well…" she began, swallowing, "I can't stop thinking about what we did that night and wondering what it meant. You and I, we…"

He held up a hand as if scared she might try to come nearer to him. "It meant *nothing*, Bailey."

"Nothing? We slept together."

He shrugged one shoulder. "We had sex. That's all it was. It shouldn't have happened. But it did. End of story. Now, if you don't mind, I've got work to do."

He gestured toward the door, dismissing her as if she were nothing more than a pesky child. Her cheeks burned, but it was a different kind of heat than before, and inside her organs felt as if they'd turned to ice. What had she been expecting? That Quinn would decorate the warehouse with balloons and crack open a bottle of expensive champagne on her return? That maybe they'd repeat their shenanigans of that fateful night?

As if. A few weeks ago, she'd been engaged to his brother. Yesterday, when she and her parents had stopped by Nora's place to wish their old friends a Happy Thanksgiving, it hadn't been the awkwardness between her and Callum that got to her, but the way Quinn had barely met her eye. Except for one question about how she knew the woman Callum had brought as his date, Quinn had barely spoken to her. And that hurt more than she'd imagined it ever could.

Was this the way things would always be between them from now on? Perhaps it would be easy if she could just walk away from the McKinnels, once and for all, but due to the friendship of their moms and the small size of Jewell Rock, that was unlikely. She could always move to Bend, the nearby town where she worked at one of the best hotels. It might only be a short drive away, but Bend was like a metropolis compared to small-town Jewell Rock, and she and Quinn would be far less likely to run into each other.

The problem was, she'd realized over the last few painful weeks, she didn't *want* to walk away from Quinn McKinnel. What had happened between them against a whiskey barrel had been explosive. Mind-blowing. Frenzied. Until then, she honestly hadn't understood all the hype about sex.

It was the thought of never experiencing that kind of sex again that had compelled her to swallow her fear and doubts and come here to face him today. To find out if he'd felt it, too. That earth-shattering, soul-changing connection, that shift inside when they'd climaxed together and she'd opened her eyes and seen him looking right into hers.

But now, looking into his eyes for one final moment, Bailey could see it had meant nothing at all to Quinn. It was clear that she was just another notch on his bedpost (or rather his whiskey barrel), and even if he wasn't such a jerk, the idea of them together was laughable. Unable to stand another moment in his presence, she turned and fled in the direction he'd pointed. She'd never felt more mortified in her life. And if she never saw Quinn McKinnel again, it would be too soon.

Chapter One

Dear Aunt Bossy:

Although I've been reading your sage advice for years, this is the first time I've ever had reason to write to you myself. And I must admit, I'm terribly ashamed to have to do so, but I'm in a quandary and I need your wisdom.

I've always been a hardworking and sensible woman who prides herself on being organized, planning ahead and making good choices. Until about two months ago, I was with a wonderful man—he was kind, dependable and hardworking—but then I lost my head. I slept with someone I shouldn't have—a sexy devil-may-care playboy who hasn't had a steady girlfriend in as long as I can remember. And I've known him all my life. Please don't think too badly of me, I already hate myself enough and the first thing I did was end my relationship.

But, as if my one-night severe lapse of judgment wasn't bad enough, somehow, despite using protection, I'm pregnant and I don't know what to do about it. Oh, I'm keeping the baby, don't get me wrong. Getting rid of it is not an option. Having a baby might not have been on my immediate agenda, but it was in my five-year plan. Granted I was hoping to be in love and married, but I can't wait to be a mom. What I'm undecided about is whether or not to tell my baby's father.

He's not the type to marry me out of a sense of obligation (at least I don't think so, and I wouldn't say yes, even if he proposed such a ridiculous arrangement), but I'm worried about him being an unsettling influence in my baby's life.

What do you think, Bossy? To tell him or not to tell him? That is my question.

Yours sincerely,

Pregnant with Mr. Wrong

Her heart beating like a brass band, Bailey read her letter over once more, glanced around the office to make sure she was alone and then pressed Print. Her stomach churning, she hurried over to the printer, snatched the piece of paper off as it shot out, and then quickly folded it up and shoved it into an envelope. With a deep breath, she took the envelope back to her desk, picked up her pen and scrawled the address of the *Bulletin* on the front. Snail mail was anonymous in a way email never truly was.

She couldn't believe her life had come to this—asking some faceless advice columnist for help—but she'd known about her pregnancy for almost a month now and was still no closer to coming to a decision about what to tell (or not to tell) Quinn.

In a cruel twist of fate, she'd discovered she was having his baby the day she had been supposed to be marrying Callum. Thank all the stars in the sky she'd broken that engagement a month before or this situation could be worse and even *more* complicated than it already was. Everyone had thought her crazy, breaking up with the oldest McKinnel brother, but they'd lost their spark—if it had ever been there in the first place—and Callum was more in love with his work at the family distillery than he'd ever been with her. He'd also met Chelsea and they were already engaged—that fact only reinforced Bailey's belief that she'd made the right decision.

But it hadn't done much for her ego. Why hadn't Callum been as head-over-heels crazy for her? Was there something wrong with her or did she just have zero talent at choosing the right guy? Either way, it didn't make her current situation any better.

Four weeks ago, when she'd first seen the two little blue lines on the pregnancy test stick, she'd gone through a roller coaster of emotions.

Shock—that fireworks hadn't been the only thing she and Quinn had created that night.

Denial—that one night, one time, when they'd used a condom, could actually result in this. Five more pregnancy tests later, she'd had to concede it had.

Terror—that she didn't know the first thing about babies. Or motherhood.

Acceptance—that whether *she* was ready or not, whether Quinn was father material or not, this was real. In eight months' time, she'd be a mom.

Excitement—that in eight months' time, her life would change irrevocably for the better, because she'd be a mom.

And then *confusion*—because…well…Quinn.

If she were honest with herself, she'd had a crush on him years ago in high school—back then pretty much every girl her age in Jewell Rock had crushed on Quinn McKinnel. He'd been *that* guy; he skipped classes, took girls down to the lake at night to make out, drove way too fast, stayed out too late and came to school hungover. He'd been like Danny in *Grease* and every girl in their year had been desperate to play Sandy. He'd dated almost every one of those girls in their final year at school. At least, it had felt like that to Bailey when she'd been standing on the sidelines watching, wishing and hoping he'd notice her.

And he hadn't slowed down any since.

But Bailey *had* grown up, and she knew that although Quinn might be charming and good in bed—*heck, yeah, he was good in bed*—he wasn't the type of guy she should fall in love with. She'd almost forgotten that in the aftermath of the best sex of her life, but he'd set her straight and made it *more* than clear. He was way too much like her father for that to be a smart idea. And the last thing she wanted for her son or daughter was an unreliable dad like she'd had. It was this fear that wreaked havoc within—ethically, she knew it was wrong to keep the baby from Quinn, but her mama bear instincts had kicked in and she wanted more for her child than she'd had. She wanted stability and love without question, without obligation—the kind of love her stepfather, Reginald, had given her and her mother, the kind of love her younger brother and sister had been born to.

She pressed her hand against her stomach, something

she'd been doing a lot these last few weeks, and closed her eyes, trying to imagine the tiny life inside. A site on the internet told her the baby was about the size of a lentil, but that its sex-defining parts were beginning to develop. Would it be a girl or a boy? Would it have dark hair and a pale complexion, like her, or dirty-blond hair and big brown eyes you could get lost in, like Quinn?

Her tummy still flat, Bailey was struggling to get her head around the fact that she was growing a real live human inside her, but she knew she was on borrowed time. Within a matter of months, she'd need a new wardrobe and would no longer be able to conceal her secret from the world.

If she decided not to tell Quinn, then she would have to come up with another story, because otherwise people would assume the baby was Callum's. And while he was without a doubt better father material than Quinn and would not hesitate to stand by her and their child, it *wasn't* his. Due to the timing of her cycle and the fact they'd drifted apart before the breakup, she knew this to be true. Thank God.

Oh, why did life have to get so complicated?

Of course, she knew the answer to that question, also. Even after their awkward meeting, Quinn had made no effort to contact her or apologize for his behavior.

Dammit, Bailey, why didn't you just get drunk or go buy a puppy or something? Wasn't that what normal people did when they were unhappy?

As a tear sneaked down her cheek, she once again contemplated the possibility of leaving town. Of starting afresh, someplace far away from Jewell Rock and Bend, someplace that wasn't populated with McKinnels. That could be the answer, but, in addition to all her reasons for wanting to remain in Jewell Rock, she'd definitely need the assistance of her family. Only what would her mom and stepdad think of this situation? They'd be so disappointed in her, and her mom was sure to tell her best friend, Nora.

No doubt both their families would weigh in on the situation, offering suggestions and eventually support—but also a sweet dosage of judgment at the fact she'd been so stupid.

And there she went again. Problems and scenarios going round and round inside her head, intensifying her morning (or rather all-day) sickness but not making anything clearer. That was why she needed the advice of Aunt Bossy. Decision made, she shoved the envelope into her purse, switched off the lights in the office, as she was the last to leave, and then headed outside into the cool January evening to her car.

Quinn poured himself a measure of his family's finest bourbon, grabbed the large yellow envelope he'd collected from the post office today, then took it and his drink across to the couch. He dumped the envelope on the coffee table, picked up his television remote with his free hand and aimed it at his big-screen TV. As the picture came to life and the sounds of tonight's basketball game filled the room, he sat down and leaned back into the couch, taking a long sip of his drink.

Ah. His family might drive him insane sometimes—arguing about what was best for their little empire—but there was no doubt about it, they knew how to make good whiskey.

It was Friday night, and while usually he'd be out on the town with the guys, carousing or actually at a game, he hadn't been in the mood for either of those options tonight. At the ripe old age of twenty-seven, maybe he was getting old.

Shaking out the contents of the package, he picked up the first letter and started to read about a woman who felt like she was playing second fiddle in her husband's life to her mother-in-law.

Marriage—how many letters about marriage problems did he receive? Those and neighborhood disputes were biggies. And while he might not have any professional qualifications to fix such issues, he had an innate talent for telling things how they were, and this woman needed to take her husband's balls in hand and give him an ultimatum.

He chuckled, looking forward to writing that letter. What had started as a dare six years ago when his friend from school was interning at the paper had become a large, important part of Quinn's life. No one, aside from his friend, who had since moved on to a much bigger newspaper in Seattle, knew that he was the writer behind the popular Aunt Bossy column. All his exchanges with the local paper were anonymous and that was the way he intended it to stay. He could just imagine the ribbing he'd get if his older brothers ever found out about his secret side business, not to mention what women might think of it, but strangely he enjoyed this gig and felt like in some bizarre way he was doing good in the world.

He took another swig of his bourbon and picked up the next letter. He was halfway through reading about a woman who found herself unexpectedly pregnant, when something about the wording gave him pause. He went back a few lines and read it again.

I slept with someone I shouldn't have—a sexy devil-may-care playboy who hasn't had a steady girlfriend in as long as I can remember. And I've known him all my life.

No. It couldn't be. He chuckled out loud at the absurdity of his thought, tossed the letter aside, took a sip of his drink and began to read the next one. But he read the first sentence about five times before he tossed *it* aside and went back to Pregnant with Mr. Wrong.

The paper starting to shake in his hand and his heart beating a mile a minute, Quinn read her letter again, over and over, and the more times he read it, the more he began to feel as if he knew the writer. *Personally. Intimately.*

His gut tightened as he thought back to that night in the warehouse when he and Bailey had consummated a relationship that wasn't meant to be. Although Pregnant with Mr. Wrong didn't go so far as to say she'd been engaged to the "good" brother, her descriptions of what happened fit his and Bailey's situation to a T. Was the devil-may-care brother with commitment issues him or was he being paranoid?

He wasn't offended by this label, as some might be— such an accusation would be true and he had good reasons for the way he was—but if it was him, there was a much bigger issue in play.

Bailey was pregnant. With his baby. He was going to be a dad. Something he had never planned on being.

His rib cage squeezing in around his heart, Quinn picked up his glass again and downed the rest of the contents. If he wasn't in such a state of shock, he'd have gotten up and walked the short distance necessary to refill it, but his brain was too full with this news to send such messages to his legs.

A baby. He and Bailey had made a baby.

Or had they? How could she be certain it was his? How could *he* be so certain this letter was from her? They'd had sex one time—granted it had been more explosive than anything he'd experienced before—but they'd used a condom. It hadn't broken, and he was pretty damn sure it hadn't been out-of-date. Didn't most people take months to get pregnant, even when they were actively trying?

This question was quickly forgotten as more of the letter sank in. In his heart of hearts he knew the letter was from her, which meant Bailey believed the baby was his and she wasn't sure whether she should tell him or not. His fist tightened around his glass and he hurled it across the room. It smashed against the wall, scattering glass all over the carpet. Now he had a mess in his house to clean up as well as a mess in his life.

But who the hell did Bailey think she was, even contemplating keeping him in the dark?

She might be the incubator, but if he was the sperm donor, as she appeared to believe, no way was she going to cut him out of their baby's life. So what if he prided himself on being the life of the party? So what if he didn't believe in the institution of marriage? So what if he'd made a decision long ago that commitment to a woman wasn't for him? That didn't mean he would shirk his responsibilities and it wasn't her right to decide he would. He thought of his brother Lachlan's ex-wife, who had walked away from her son—he would never, could never, do that, and it riled him that had he not read this letter, Bailey might have made that decision for him.

What made her think she would be a better parent than he would, anyway? His dating history had no bearing on this issue.

Enraged, Quinn stood. Abandoning the other letters and the broken glass, he strode toward his front door, where he grabbed his leather jacket, helmet and motorcycle keys before storming out of the house. Thankfully he'd had only one drink, so he was safe to ride.

The bitter winter wind sliced into his cheeks, burning his skin, as he rode the short distance to Bailey's apartment block on the other side of Jewell Rock, but consumed with anger, he barely registered it.

Just wait till he saw her. He revved the engine and took a curve fast, suddenly realizing just how much his life was about to change.

Late nights on the town would be exchanged for long nights walking up and down the hallway with a restless baby—he'd been around enough when his nephew, Hamish, was little to know what the future held. He could kiss goodbye to sleeping in on the weekends, and perhaps he'd have to exchange this bike for a more family-friendly vehicle, something that had room for car seats.

His chest tightening at the enormity of it all, he slowed the bike in front of Bailey's town house and parked. Fueled by a weird cocktail of fury and fervor, he strode toward the building, ready to confront her—to find out if it were true that she was pregnant with his kid.

Moments later, he lifted his fist and rapped hard on her front door, tapping his boot on the floor as he waited for her to answer. That wait seemed like an eternity, but after a few minutes he finally heard footsteps approaching, and then the door peeled open. Bailey stood there in pink flannel pajamas, her eyes and mouth wide-open, as if he were the last person she expected to see, and her hair wet, as if she'd just stepped out of the shower.

"Quinn?"

If he'd had any doubt in his heart that Bailey was pregnant, one look at her eradicated that possibility. She looked utterly exhausted, yet at the same time she glowed. Bailey with her pale skin, cute button nose, sleek black hair and luscious curves had always been beautiful in a classic kind of way, but in this moment she took his breath away. He couldn't think of any woman as gorgeous as she was and something shifted inside him.

"Quinn?" she said again. "What are you doing here?"

He opened his mouth to tell her that he knew and to ask her what the heck crazy game she was playing at. But the words caught in his throat as two awful thoughts struck. Confronting her would expose Aunt Bossy, but more important, did he really want his baby to be welcomed into the world by feuding parents?

His mind drifted to his niece and nephew. Or, more to the point, to his sweet niece, who because of her parents' bitter divorce was shuffled between her dad, who lived in Jewell Rock, and her mom, who lived in Bend, while her twin brother lived permanently with his dad. Quinn didn't want that conflicted life for his kid. He wanted only the best for his baby and that meant two parents, all of the time—even if that went against all the rules he lived by.

He rubbed the side of his jaw, racking his mind for a reply. However angry he might be at Bailey, however misguided she was, he understood one thing. And that was that her intentions were honorable—the desire to love and protect their baby. Two minutes ago he wouldn't have considered marriage if someone had offered him a billion dollars, but now, seeing the vulnerability in her eyes as she stood in front of him, imagining the new life growing inside her, he wanted to love and protect their baby, as well. And the most logical solution was getting married so they could parent one hundred percent together.

But Bailey had made it clear in her letter that she wouldn't marry the Quinn she knew simply because they were going to be parents.

So, it was his job to show her the side of himself she didn't know—the side that knew, if he was given half a chance, he could take care of both her and their baby.

Bailey's glare, followed by her attempt to shut the door in his face, reminded him he'd been staring at her, possibly for minutes. He put his foot out to stop the door closing and summoned his most charming smile. "I've got a proposition for you."

Chapter Two

What the heck was Quinn doing on her doorstep on a Friday night? Bailey wondered. Didn't he have someplace better to be? Like a bar, hitting on anything with a skirt.

Her heart thrashed wildly at the sight of him, wearing faded jeans, a long-sleeved white T-shirt and a leather jacket that should be an illegal combo where he was concerned. His hair was mussed up from his helmet, which only amplified his sex appeal. Her mouth went dry and her grip on the door loosened as he nudged it open again with his boot-clad foot and hit her with a smile that left her dizzy.

And what had he just said about a proposition? She couldn't voice any of these questions because her tongue had tied when her eyes locked with his dark, dangerous gaze. Not dangerous because he would ever physically hurt her, but because when she looked into those big brown pools of seduction, it wasn't only her heart that quivered.

And any kind of visceral reaction to this guy was a bad idea.

Yet here he was, standing before her looking hotter than any man should have a right to, and she was standing before *him* wearing her favorite old pj's that had seen better days, feeling as if she might collapse from exhaustion at any moment. She hoped she didn't have sauce on her chin from the pizza she'd all but scoffed.

Maybe this is a nightmare, she thought as her hand drifted up to wipe her face. Maybe in her early-pregnancy fatigue she'd come home, collapsed on the couch and fallen into a deep slumber that had led her straight to him. Since the news of the baby, her thoughts had never drifted far from him, no matter how much she tried to direct them elsewhere.

She pinched herself. It hurt, and Quinn frowned down at her odd behavior.

"Are you okay?" He reached out a hand and laid it gently on her arm.

Bailey flinched, not because it didn't feel good—damn her hussy hormones—but because she couldn't let down her guard. She and Quinn hadn't spoken since that awful day after Thanksgiving, and she couldn't think of any logical reason for his sudden appearance now. Unless… *he knew.*

Her errantly beating heart stopped altogether for a few long moments. A chill spread over her at this impossible thought. *No.* She hadn't told anyone except the doctor in Bend (where she'd chosen to go in case anyone in Jewell Rock saw her at the hospital) and the local paper's advice columnist. She thought of the letter she'd scribbled and hastily posted yesterday afternoon—Aunt Bossy might not even have it yet, and it certainly hadn't appeared in the paper, so… She needed to take a chill pill before Quinn suspected something was off aside from the awkwardness that already simmered between them.

"I'm fine. You're just the last person I expected to see." She wrapped her arms tightly around herself and stared at him expectantly, trying to channel the look he'd given her when he'd all but thrown her out of the warehouse. "Did you say something about a proposition?"

"Are you going to ask me inside?"

She swallowed at the thought of being alone in her apartment with all six feet of Quinn McKinnel. He was without a doubt the sexiest of the five McKinnel brothers—that was quite a feat—and he knew it. From the way he swaggered when he walked, to the way he wore that leather jacket like leather had been invented for him, to the way he smiled at all the local ladies…he *knew* it.

Callum had always joked that whenever Quinn stepped into the tasting room at the distillery, their sales hit the roof. He just had to smile at a potential *female* buyer and they fell over their own feet in their hurry to buy Mc-Kinnel's famed whiskey.

Maybe he'd changed his mind? Maybe he was looking for a hookup? Desire curled low in her belly at that ridiculous thought and she almost laughed out loud. He might be all about no-strings-attached sex—he'd made *that* clear in those few postcoital moments—but she could never be that girl. Especially not now there was another little person involved. Her hand went to her stomach instinctively; she didn't even notice until his eyes followed it.

"Are you not well?"

"I'm fine. Why wouldn't I be?" She snapped her hand back and stepped aside, gesturing for him to come in. The last thing she needed was one of her neighbors seeing him and starting rumors.

Quinn raised one sexy shoulder as he stepped inside and shut the door behind them. He was so close she could smell the well-worn leather of his jacket and just a hint of whiskey. All the McKinnels smelled of whiskey—not in an alcoholic I've-drunk-too-much kinda way, but in a way she guessed folks who worked and owned a distillery would. Quinn managed the warehouse, which, because he was hands-on in *every* aspect of his life, she guessed involved a lot of heavy lifting and manual labor, just one of the things that contributed to his muscular physique.

"Can I get you a drink?" she asked, trying to lure her thoughts from the way he'd been hands-on with her, and hoping he'd decline and simply get to the point about what was so urgent that it couldn't wait until the morning. Or couldn't be conveyed in a telephone call.

He smiled. "You look tired. How about *I* make you a drink? What do you want? Coffee?"

Befuddled by his offer, she shook her head. "No, if I drink caffeine at this time, I'll be up all night." *And I'm steering clear because of the baby.* The last month had been torturous without her morning coffee hit, not to mention her midday and afternoon ones. Lack of caffeine on top of the dreaded morning sickness made every day difficult.

"I'll see what I can find. You go sit." And Quinn actually put his hands on her shoulders, swiveled her around and gave her a light push in the direction of her lounge room. Despite the layer of flannel protection, awareness skittered across her skin at his touch.

Bailey could already hear him clattering about in her tiny kitchen by the time she flopped down onto the couch. Her eyes landed on a pile of magazines on her coffee table—three copies of *Vogue* and one about pregnancy. *Sheesh!* She leaned forward, snatched up the magazine and shoved it under the cushion on which she sat. She'd picked it up yesterday on her lunch break and had been careful to keep it in her bag so no one at the hotel where she worked saw it, but she hadn't considered the need to hide things in her own home.

As she took deep breaths in and out, she glanced around for anything else that might give her state away. Thank God the pregnancy test kit was long gone, and when Quinn saw the empty pizza box in the kitchen, he'd likely just think her a lazy glutton. If she didn't slow down on the eating front, she'd be the size of a cow by the time this baby arrived.

She needed to spend less time eating and more time tidying her apartment, she thought as she took in the chaos around her. Her apartment, which was normally neat and ordered, was anything but that right now. Exactly like her life. How had everything gone so downhill so quickly?

Hopefully Quinn, who hadn't been inside in a long while, wouldn't notice anything amiss. Tapping her sock-clad feet on the carpet, she frowned as a noise like the blender started up in her kitchen. What on earth was he doing in there? While part of her wanted to get up and go check, her eyelids felt so heavy and the couch was too comfortable. She curled her legs up beside her and...

"He's always working. He never wants to spend any time with me. We're supposed to be getting married in

under two months and he can't even find the time to talk
to me about it." Bailey hated crying, hated sounding so
needy, but now the words were spilling from her lips, and
she couldn't seem to stop them.

"He's a fool," Quinn said, sliding his hand up her neck
and into her hair. He twisted her head so they were looking into each other's eyes. The way he looked at her sent
ripples of awareness through her, and for a second she
forgot what she was so upset about. All she could think
about was how close he was and how good he smelled.

"You're gorgeous, Bails," he whispered, his hot palm
still resting against her bare neck. "Don't let anyone ever
make you feel otherwise."

Her nipples tingled as she wished his hands on them,
as well. Then, as if he were a genie granting her every
desire, he leaned forward and kissed the lone tear that,
in her rage and upset, had trickled down her cheek.

He pulled back, and their eyes met again as he licked
his lips, tasting her on them. They stared at each other a
few long moments, Bailey's heart was pounding so hard
she'd have sworn he could hear it, as well. And then
he dipped his head and kissed her again. This time full
on the lips. All notions of right and wrong flew out the
window. All Bailey could think about was how amazing
Quinn's lips felt on hers.

He dropped his hands to her ass and pulled her tighter
against him, kissing her like she'd only ever dreamed of
being kissed. Having been neglected of late, her hormones stood to attention, begging her to up the ante and
kiss him back.

A tiny voice in the depths of her mind tried to tell her
that getting naked with him wasn't a good idea, but Bailey ignored it, helping Quinn by shrugging off her jacket

as he pushed it down over her shoulders. The blouse she'd been wearing for work came next. Their mouths parted as he whipped it over her head and she shivered momentarily as the cool evening air hit her skin.

Not a word was said between them. Not a thought to where they were and who might happen to stumble upon them. Instead, Quinn dipped his head and took one of her nipples into his mouth. Despite the lace of her bra, she bit down on a shriek as he twirled his tongue around her bud, the sensations shooting right to her core.

"God, Quinn." She reached out to steady herself on his shoulders as he took her other nipple and gave it equal attention. With each flick of his tongue, he drove her a little more insane, a little more desperate. She wanted him, she needed him. Not just his mouth on her, but all of him, inside her.

She reached her hand out and slid it down the front of his trousers. He groaned as her fingers closed around the prize, his warmth and hardness only increasing her desire. She was wet for him, her knees shaking, her toes quivering and her breath coming hard and fast in anticipation.

He snapped his head back up and kissed her again, simultaneously raking her skirt up to her hips. Unsteady on her feet, she leaned back against a whiskey barrel for support and spread her legs, desperate for his touch. And Quinn gave her exactly what she wanted. He hooked one finger beneath her panties and slid the finger inside her. All it took was a few deft strokes and his mouth back on her nipple, and she was panting like she'd never panted before.

As the pressure built up inside her, all she could think about was having him. "Do you have a condom?" she whispered.

In reply, he conjured one out of his back pocket and held it up. Of course Jewell Rock's chief Casanova would carry a condom. While she snatched the little foil packet and ripped it open with her teeth, Quinn yanked down his trousers. Smiling like someone about to win the lottery, she reached for his naked erection and rolled on the protection.

Then, also grinning, Quinn lifted her atop the barrel and removed her panties, dropping them to the floor beside them. Desperate, Bailey wrapped her legs around him and anchored her hands on his shoulders, her head falling back as he thrust into her.

"Bailey? Bailey?"

She blinked her eyes open and shook her head, shooting up into a sitting position at the sound of Quinn's voice. He was perched on the edge of her coffee table, only a foot or so away from her, holding out a large glass with white liquid inside. How long had she been out cold?

Long enough to have a sordid dream.

Her cheeks burned and she hoped he couldn't read her mind.

"What is that?" she asked, her tone perhaps a tad accusatory, but having Quinn so close set her on edge. Awareness and guilt warred within her.

"It's a vanilla milk shake."

"You made me a *milk shake*?" She couldn't keep the surprise from her voice as she reached out to take it from him, careful not to let their fingers touch in the exchange.

He cocked his head to one side and smiled that toe-curling grin. "Well, you said you didn't want coffee. I couldn't find the ingredients for hot chocolate and you don't like tea, but of course you had ice cream."

"You remembered I don't like tea?" The surprises just kept coming.

He nodded, his gaze trained on hers. "Of course. We're friends, aren't we? Friends remember each other's likes and dislikes."

She swallowed. *Friends?* Was that what they were? Friends with benefits? Friends who accidentally made a mistake and slept together? Friends who just happened to have conceived a baby?

"Thank you," she managed and then took a sip of her drink. The cool sweetness slid down her throat. The man was not only hot and good in bed, but he could also make a mean milk shake.

"Did you make one for yourself?" she asked, leaning back into the couch, trying to look relaxed—even though she felt anything but.

"No. And I won't keep you long. You look exhausted."

"Jeez, thanks. Way to make a girl feel good."

"Looking exhausted is not mutually exclusive to looking gorgeous, not where you're concerned, anyway."

Her insides heated at his compliment, but common sense immediately reminded her that sweet-talking was simply Quinn's way. It didn't *mean* anything. "Why are you here, anyway?"

He cleared his throat, and dammit, even that sounded sexy. "Well…um…" She'd never heard him sound anything but confident before and this stammering was strangely endearing.

"Yes?" she prodded, wishing he'd just spit it out and leave. Somehow, while she'd been dating and then engaged to Callum, she'd managed to control her attraction to his younger brother. But now that she and Quinn had done the horizontal mambo, she couldn't be within twenty feet of him without remembering how explosive they'd been together. Even the thought of how he'd treated her afterward, even the thought of his baby inside her wasn't enough of a cold shower.

"You probably know it's my mom's sixtieth birthday soon?"

"Of course." Before she'd ended her engagement, Bailey had been trying to work out the perfect present for her future mother-in-law's big six-oh, but now she wasn't sure Nora would want anything from her.

"As you know, the last six months hasn't been easy on her. Hell, it hasn't been easy on any of us, but I don't want to let this slide by without a celebration. My family's all so busy with the building of the new restaurant and Callum's expansion plans that I was wondering if you would organize a party for her?"

He didn't mention his dad's death in the equation, but Bailey suddenly wondered if grief over the shocking loss of his father was part of the reason Quinn had broken the rules and slept with her. Maybe none of them had been thinking straight.

When she hesitated, he added, "We'd pay you, of course. I just want to do something really special for Mom."

She'd been going to refuse, but his heartfelt words and obvious love for his mother got to her. And, if she were honest, surprised her. Also, this was the grandmother of her baby they were talking about. She felt guilty enough about her secret, but, even if she did come clean eventually, right now it was too soon after she and Callum had broken up. She needed time to get her head around this situation herself and didn't want to be the cause of family disharmony, so perhaps the least she could do was help make Nora's birthday special.

"And," Quinn continued, sounding like a salesman who thought he was in danger of losing a sale, "it'll be a chance for you to show the others your impeccable talent for creating magical events. That way, when the restaurant opens and we start holding functions at the distillery, everyone will be more favorably disposed to throw the business your way. I know you were interested in the McKinnel event contract."

She *was* interested in working with the famed McKinnel distillery—was, as in past tense, pre-baby. Now she wasn't so sure working in such close proximity to Quinn was a good idea. He did crazy things to her insides. Then again, just because he'd approached her, just because he'd be paying the bills for the birthday bash, didn't mean they'd need to spend much time together. Attending parties might be Quinn's thing, but he generally left the organizing to others.

"Okay. What kind of event were you thinking?"

He slowly shrugged those big sexy shoulders and she tried not to stare. "Intimate but special. A few of her closest friends and family. A band, maybe a small dance floor. I was thinking we could hire a small marquee and hold the party at the distillery. If it's still cold, we'll also hire some heaters for the marquee. I'm sure Lachlan would be interested in catering and testing out some of his new recipes."

"You haven't asked him yet?"

He rubbed his lips one over the other. "I wanted to run the idea past you first."

"Why me? There are other event planners in the vicinity."

"Because you're the best."

The way he said *best*, and the way he stared intently at her as he did so, wreaked havoc with her already errant hormones. It was almost as if he wasn't simply referring to her work, but that thought was ridiculous. She tried to push it out of her mind.

"Flattery will get you everywhere," she joked.

His lips curled into another grin. "Is that a yes?"

She nodded while silently questioning her sanity. "Have you decided on a date yet?"

"How about we meet for lunch tomorrow and talk details then? You can tell me what else you need from me to get started."

Lunch? He sounded like he might be a whole lot more involved in the planning than she'd imagined. Her stomach flipped at the thought of spending too much time with Quinn, but maybe working with him to organize this party would help her body and her hormones settle down. Because if she *did* tell him about the baby, they'd be linked forever and she'd need to be able to talk to him about their child's welfare without harboring a head full of dirty thoughts.

"Sure, lunch sounds great. Why don't we meet in Bend and we can choose a theme and then go to the stationers to select the invitations." Needing to keep in control of this situation, she made it sound like a statement, not a question. If they met in Bend, it would also be less likely that they'd be seen together by someone who knew them.

"I'll swing by and pick you up on my way."

"No." That would make it more like a date—not that Quinn McKinnel did dating, but she needed to protect her own emotions. And being squished against Quinn on the back of his motorcycle would be like throwing her emotions to the piranhas. This was purely a business deal. "I'll probably do some shopping before or after." She named a lesser-known café in Bend and a time.

For a moment Quinn looked as if he might argue about not picking her up, but in the end he conceded. "Okay. Thanks. I'll see you tomorrow." He pushed himself off the coffee table and towered above her. Lord, he was tall—all the McKinnels were tall *and* good-looking, but if they were giving out awards, he'd win.

She put down her milk shake and went to stand.

"No, don't get up." He put out a hand to stop her. "I'll see myself out. You get some rest. I'll see you tomorrow."

Too tired to fight, Bailey let Quinn go and thankfully fatigue consumed her so that she fell asleep quickly and didn't have time to worry or think about Quinn, the baby or what she'd just agreed to do.

"Well, hello there." Callum looked up from behind the tasting bar as Quinn strolled toward him. He had the smug smile on his face—the smile that had been permanently in place since he'd shacked up with Chelsea—and Quinn guessed that one word about the baby would wipe it off. He'd have to tell his brother eventually, but announcing he'd gotten Bailey pregnant was probably not the smartest news to divulge when she hadn't even told him yet.

Especially as he was still coming to terms with it himself.

Usually, he'd still be in bed at this time on a Saturday morning, but he hadn't been able to sleep, his head too full with thoughts of Bailey, thoughts of a baby and thoughts of whether or not he really had it in him to be the type of dad he wanted to be.

"We don't usually see you round here on the weekend," Callum said as he rubbed at a smudge on the bar with the cuff of his shirt.

Since the warehouse shut down on the weekends, Quinn got Saturdays and Sundays off, whereas Callum and his other siblings who worked at the distillery—Sophie and Blair—worked pretty much 24/7. But that was their choice; he wasn't going to be made to feel guilty about his. Their dad had been a workaholic (among other things) and in no way did Quinn want to emulate him. Ever since he was sixteen and walked in on his dad fucking a woman who wasn't his mom, Quinn had vowed to never be like his father. But, in sleeping with Bailey, who hadn't been available at the time, he'd been just like him.

And now they both needed to face the consequences.

"Is Sophie around?" he asked, ignoring his older brother's observation.

"She's grabbing coffees," Callum said, jerking his thumb down the corridor in the direction of their small staff kitchen.

Before Quinn could say anything more, their sister appeared carrying two steaming mugs. Although she looked surprised to see him, unlike Callum she didn't verbalize this surprise.

"Hey." She handed Callum his coffee and then stretched up on tippy-toes and kissed Quinn on the cheek. "How are you today, brother mine?"

He forced a smile. "I'm surviving. And you?"

"Much the same. What brings you in here?" she asked, not sounding accusatory in the slightest.

"I wanted to let you guys know I'm organizing a surprise party for Mom's sixtieth."

"Oh, that's a wonderful idea." The smile on Sophie's face showed her approval.

Callum raised an eyebrow. "And you didn't think to run this by the rest of us first?"

"I'm telling you now," Quinn said, knowing his brother was only annoyed because he hadn't been the one to think up the brilliant idea. "I'm also telling you that I've commissioned Bailey Sawyer to plan it for me."

Sophie blinked at this news and Callum's eyes looked positively dark.

Before either of them could say anything, Quinn spoke again. "You know she's good and we agreed to throw some of our new event business her way. I thought this was as good a place as any to start. I'm meeting her for lunch later today, so let me know if you have any special requests for the party and I'll pass them on."

At that moment the door opened and their first customers waltzed in, bringing a gush of cool winter air with them. Their eyes lit up at the sight of the log fire crackling in the middle of one wall, and Sophie went over to greet them.

"Welcome to McKinnel's Distillery," she said in her eternally friendly tone. "Cool day out there. Warm yourselves by the fire and allow me to fetch you a taste of our finest bourbon to heat your insides."

"What game are you playing at, Quinn?" Callum asked, his voice low as Sophie wooed the gray-haired couple.

Truth was, Quinn didn't know what game he was playing at—he was making it up as he went along. Last night, when he'd stormed over to Bailey's place, the last thing he'd expected was to ask her help to throw a party, but then she'd looked so tired and vulnerable, and something inside him had shifted. A party for his mom had been the first excuse that came into his head when she'd asked why he was there.

He held up his hands in surrender. "I don't know what you're talking about. I'm just trying to do something special for Mom."

Callum's expression said he didn't buy this excuse for one second. Well, Quinn didn't care—as long as Bailey did. He needed to spend as much time as possible with her. He needed to win her trust and respect so that she would feel comfortable inviting him into her life—and their baby's.

"Are you interested in Bailey?"

Quinn crossed his arms and tried to ignore the guilt he felt at Callum's accusatory tone. "What if I was?"

"I'd tell you to be careful," Callum replied, his serious eyes meeting Quinn's.

He couldn't tell if his big brother was warning him off for his well-being or for Bailey's; probably the latter, but either way he could take a hike. Callum had had a chance with Bailey and he'd blown it—if he hadn't made her feel so alone and unloved, she wouldn't have come crying to Quinn in the first place. But he had and she did.

Now Callum was with Chelsea, and Bailey was Quinn's business—even if no one knew it yet.

"You worry too much," Quinn said, reaching out and patting Callum patronizingly on the chest. Inside he didn't feel so light and carefree, but he played the part expected of him. "You should be putting all your energies into your gorgeous future wife."

The fight in Callum's eyes dimmed at the mention of Chelsea, and Quinn took the chance to escape. "Now, if you don't mind, I've got things to do."

Callum opened his mouth as if to state his objections, but Quinn walked away, knowing that Callum would never make a scene when they had customers. "Bye, Sophie." He waved as he headed for the door, then stepped out into the chilly morning air and strode over to his bike.

Next stop was his mom's house, only a short distance from the actual distillery, also on their family's estate. He'd lived there with his parents and all six of his siblings growing up, but now his dad was gone and only two of his brothers still lived at home. Lachlan had moved back in with his newborn son years ago when his wife had left them. Mom loved having her grandson under her roof, and Lachlan had been grateful for her help. Blair had moved home two years ago when he'd split with his wife, who'd also been his high school sweetheart. Although he kept making noises about moving into a place of his own, Quinn reckoned he liked Mom's home cooking too much.

He parked his bike out front, hooked his helmet on the handlebars, walked the small distance to the house and let himself inside. The smell of blueberry pancakes hit him immediately, and his stomach growled in enthusiastic anticipation.

"Looks like I arrived just in time," he said as he entered the big, country-style kitchen to find his mom laying the pancakes on the table. Lachlan and his son, Hamish, sat at the other end playing chess.

"Morning, sweetheart," Nora said as Quinn hugged her. "Has your stomach got some kind of homing beacon on it?"

He laughed and then went over to ruffle Hamish's hair. "Hey, dude, how's it hanging?"

"Hi, Uncle Quinn." Hamish's words slurred slightly as usual. "I'm beating Dad at chess. Want a game?"

Quinn's heart swelled with love and pride for his nephew, who, with cerebral palsy, hadn't had an easy time in his short life but was always happy and positive. A lot of that was to do with his dad; none of the credit could go to his mother, who hadn't been able to handle a special-needs child.

"Why not?" he said. "But I warn you, I'm worse than your father."

"Hey!" Lachlan objected, a grin on his face. "Anyway, to what do we owe the pleasure?"

As his mom had turned back to the stove, Quinn moved closer to his brother and whispered, "I want to talk to you about Mom's birthday. Where's Blair?"

"In the shower, then I think he's heading over to the distillery to run a tour."

Quinn devoured four pancakes, chatted to his mom, brother and nephew about stuff Hamish was learning at school, lost a game of chess, and then stood and made his excuses. "I've got to head into Bend for a meeting. I'll catch you all later." He made eye contact with Lachlan, indicating he should see him out.

"*You've* got a meeting?" Nora asked.

He smiled at her. "Don't sound so surprised." Then he leaned down to kiss her on the forehead, before exiting the kitchen.

Lachlan followed. "I'll see Quinn out," he called over his shoulder.

Once they were safely outside, Quinn relayed his party plans.

"That's a great idea," Lachlan said, not making any comment about Bailey's involvement. "And of course I'll cater." He had that gleam in his eyes he got whenever he was talking about food, and Quinn could tell he was already conjuring up a menu. "So that's what your meeting is about? You're seeing Bailey?"

Quinn nodded once and hoped Lachlan didn't notice his Adam's apple move slowly up and down. He felt bad lying to Lachlan, although technically he wasn't. "Can you fill Blair in when you see him? I'll try to catch Annabel this afternoon."

"I'm glad you're getting her involved."

"Who? Annabel?" Of course he'd include their sister in any decisions.

"No, idiot. Bailey."

"Ah. Right."

"She's been such a big part of the family for so long, even before she and Callum were together, that it seems wrong not to have her around anymore. Callum's moved on and it was her decision to end things, so I'm just hoping everything won't have to change too much. Hamish misses her, our families are so linked, and I think hiring Bailey to help is a good plan to fix any rifts caused by her breaking up with Callum. Is she cool with helping now Chelsea is on the scene?"

Quinn had no idea what Bailey thought of Callum's new fiancée—their night had happened before all that and he'd steered clear of her since—but he guessed Chelsea was the least of her problems now. "Yes, seems to be. Bailey's a professional."

Lachlan nodded. "Yes, you're right. She is."

For a moment Quinn considered confiding in his brother—he and Lachlan had always been closer than he and Callum, and as Lachlan was a dad, he'd be more likely to understand the mixed feelings consuming Quinn right now. Panic, guilt, anger—he had them all. He wanted to ask how Lachlan had felt when he'd first discovered his ex-wife was pregnant. If he'd ever doubted his abilities as a father. If he instinctively knew what to do when his babies were first placed in his arms. If there was any parenting how-to book he absolutely should buy.

But he swallowed his questions, summoned a carefree grin onto his face and punched Lachlan playfully on the arm. "We'll chat soon and Bailey will probably be in contact, as well."

"Okay, I'll look forward to it."

As his brother slipped back inside the house, Quinn wondered how Bailey had managed to keep her pregnancy a secret so far, because he'd known less than twenty-four hours and was already desperate to confide in someone.

Chapter Three

Arriving early, Quinn paused outside the café in downtown Bend and peered in through the window, checking to see if Bailey had arrived yet. He immediately located her at a table in the corner, leaning over a newspaper as if it had the answers to world peace scrawled across the pages.

And man, she was beautiful. Her dark, shiny hair fell slightly across her eyes, and without the pajamas of last night, she was back to her immaculately dressed self—black leggings, knee-high boots to match a long knit sweater thing, bright chunky jewelry hanging around her neck. She looked together, refreshed and *pregnant*.

No one else might be able to tell, but to him the differences were obvious. Her skin definitely glowed, and even from this vantage point, he noted her breasts had increased at least a cup size. Quinn swallowed at the recollection of exactly how those breasts had felt in his hands, her nipples growing tight as he'd swiped his tongue over the top of them. He hadn't had sex like that in a long time.

Quinn caught himself. Was this the way he should be thinking about the mother of his *child*? Despite the cool temperature of the day, a flush crawled up his neck at the thought. Then again, maybe this was exactly the way he should be thinking—it wouldn't be a hardship getting serious with Bailey, as his libido was already a hundred percent behind the idea. He might not have planned on committing to anyone, but he'd make damn sure he never did to his child what his dad had done to him. And that meant doing right by the kid's mother.

The door to the café opened as a group of women emerged, giggling. He straightened as they all paused to give him the once-over. The two blondes, the brunette and the redhead were dressed as if they'd just come from a dance club or yoga class. Normally, presented with four hot women, he'd take a moment to flirt a little and get a phone number or two for his little black book, but today he barely gave them a second glance.

As they giggled off down the sidewalk, Quinn turned back to look at Bailey. She was still engrossed in the newspaper, but pretty soon she'd start wondering where he was. He couldn't remember feeling nervous about anything in his life, but his stomach was churning and his palms sweating.

Nothing had ever mattered as much as this did. He couldn't afford to mess it up.

Telling himself to get a grip, Quinn strode the few steps to the door and pulled it open. He made a beeline for Bailey, but she didn't look up until his shadow fell across the table. He glanced down at the newspaper and saw exactly what had captured her attention.

"Hello, Bailey."

"Oh. Hi, Quinn." She looked up at him, slammed the paper shut and then shot him a guilty grin, as if she'd been caught in a criminal act. "Have a seat."

She failed dismally in sounding professional and he smiled knowingly as he unwrapped his thick scarf from around his neck. He folded and placed it over the back of the vacant chair, then peeled off his leather jacket and did the same with it. He didn't think much about the act of doing so, but Bailey's eyes widened as if he were some stripper in a male revue and her cheeks grew pink when he caught her looking. It appeared the attraction was still very much present for both of them and the knowledge pleased him immensely.

If Bailey thought she could fight this kind of chemistry, she had another think coming. If she thought he wasn't going to be involved in his kid's life, she needed her pretty little head read.

"Sorry I'm late," he said. *I would have been early except I was outside giving myself a hard-on by looking in at you.* How was it possible to be angry with and attracted to someone at the same time?

She shook her head. "You're not. You're right on time." She sounded surprised by this fact and he had an urge to reach out and tuck the hair that had fallen across her face behind her ear. Then to swipe his thumb across her forehead and smooth her creased brow.

Instead, he gestured to the closed newspaper between them. "Was that Aunt Bossy you were reading?" he asked, casually picking it up. He opened it exactly to that page and smiled down at the caricature of an old woman that topped his popular column—the image about as unlike him as you could get.

Bailey's face turned a pale shade of green. "You know about Aunt Bossy?"

He shrugged one shoulder slowly as he leaned back in his seat. "Of course. Who doesn't? I read her column every week. She sounds like a very wise woman, offers top-notch advice in my opinion." He shut his mouth before she got suspicious about his effusive praise.

Now, in addition to her sickly pallor, panic danced in her eyes. "Really?" she whispered.

Yes, Bailey, I read the column and so does almost everyone else in Jewell Rock and all the surrounding regions.

Really, what had she been thinking sending such a letter? Did she think no one would recognize their situation? Their illicit night together might still be secret, but with the other clues she'd sown, it wouldn't be too hard for anyone who knew them both to put two and two together. Especially once she started to show. That was if he chose to write a public reply, something he hadn't decided yet.

This would be the perfect moment to come clean. He could add flippantly that *if* Aunt Bossy replied to her letter (and she didn't have time to reply to every one she got), the answer wouldn't appear until next week's edition at the earliest, and then he'd watch as realization dawned.

Maybe he *should* just tell her the truth. Take the high ground and demand she marry him. But there were two major problems with that scenario: one, she'd know he was Aunt Bossy, and two, she'd refuse his proposal on the grounds he didn't love her, but would start calling the shots anyway. Bailey didn't excel at event planning for no reason; she was born a control freak and he wasn't about to be pushed about by anyone. Not when his baby was involved.

The way he was playing things might be untoward, but he needed Bailey to confide in him on her own terms, or at least think she was.

While he deliberated, she recovered her shock and said, "I thought you only opened the paper for the sports news."

It was supposed to be an insult and he felt it twist inside him like barbed wire, but he refused to let his hurt show. "Just goes to show you don't know everything about me, Bailey Sawyer," he said, his tone half amused, half suggestive.

Her eyes widened, color darkened her cheeks and for a second there he thought she was going to confess, but before she could say anything, a waitress with a badge announcing her as Daphne appeared at their table.

"Hey, y'all." She obviously didn't come from around here. "What can I get for you?"

Quinn looked to Bailey; Bailey looked to the waitress. "Can you give us a few more moments?"

All smiles, Daphne nodded and retreated. Bailey picked up the menu and Quinn did the same. It took him all of two seconds to decide on the chicken gorgonzola sandwich, but Bailey deliberated longer than she usually did over anything. He watched her brow furrowed in serious contemplation and wondered what she was thinking? Was she trying to work out if there was anything on the menu pregnant women shouldn't eat? Or was she feeling queasy?

He'd been up half the night researching pregnancy on the internet, so he could have helped her make an informed decision, but as he'd already established he wasn't ready to come clean, he sat patiently waiting while she made her choice. The second she put down her menu, Daphne swooped back to the table and smiled again, her pen poised over her pad ready.

"I'll have the veggie frittata, please, and a Diet Coke," Bailey said.

"Good choice." The waitress scribbled, then looked to Quinn.

Before he could give his order, Bailey spoke again. "Actually, scrap the Diet Coke, I'll have a club soda instead."

He smiled his approval. She was doing everything she could to protect their baby. Including keeping him at a distance. This last thought killed his smile.

"Okay. Sure." The waitress looked to Quinn. "And what can I get for you?"

Quinn ordered his sandwich and was glad when the other woman retreated. "Thanks for agreeing to meet me today," he said, "especially on a weekend." He stretched his legs out, pretending the brush against Bailey's legs was accidental.

"It's a pleasure," she said, snapping her legs away from his, her cheeks reddening again. "Now, shall we get started?" Without waiting for a reply, she got out her notebook, diary and a pink pen and got straight down to business. "First things first. Have you got a date in mind?"

"Well, her birthday is March fifteenth, so I guess a weekend either side of that. What works best for you?"

Bailey stuck her pen between her teeth as she flicked through the pages of her diary. "We've got Saturday the eleventh or Saturday the eighteenth? I'm free either. Have you checked with…with your brothers and sisters yet?"

"Yep—I've spoken to everyone this morning. They're really excited. And happy that you're going to be involved."

She raised an eyebrow. "Really? *All* of them?"

He reached across the table and took her hand—he could tell the action surprised her, but he didn't retreat and neither did she. Her skin felt soft and her hand fit perfectly in his. "Yes. We all consider you part of the family. No one wants the fact that you've broken up with Callum to change that."

Or what happened between you and me.

He could tell by the way her gaze met his and her cheeks turned slightly redder that she was also thinking about that night. She rubbed her lips one over the other and finally removed her hand. "Okay. Well, let's go with the eleventh. If you want it to be a surprise, before the actual date is always better. She's less likely to get suspicious or think you've all forgotten her birthday."

Quinn chuckled. "I don't think Mom would ever let us forget."

The first smile of the day cracked across Bailey's face. "No, Nora definitely wouldn't let that happen. She's going to be delighted by all this. I have a list of questions to ask you to give me a better idea of what you want. Ready?"

He nodded, although party plans were pretty low down on the list of things he'd like to be discussing with her right now.

"We've chosen a date, so next is the time of day. I'm guessing you'd prefer an evening event when the distillery has closed?"

Truthfully, he hadn't given the finer details any thought, but he nodded all the same. He'd pretty much go along with whatever she suggested where the party was concerned, but he didn't plan on being so obliging about their baby. "Sounds good. Say, about seven o'clock?"

Bailey scribbled that down. "You'll have to work out how to get Nora out of the way for the afternoon while we set up."

"I'll put Annabel and Sophie in charge of that. They can invite her out for a late lunch or something."

"Good thinking," Bailey said as Daphne arrived with their drinks.

"Your meals won't be long," she promised, before turning back to the kitchen.

Bailey took a sip of her club soda and immediately returned to business. "Do you want a theme?"

"What? Like fancy dress?"

"I was thinking more like a special color or motif. You know, like butterflies, her favorite flower or something. But fancy dress could be fun." She paused a few moments, then her eyes positively sparkled. "She was born in 1957, right? So let's have a 1950s theme."

"What? Like 1950s glamour?" Quinn imagined Bailey dressed as Audrey Hepburn, who had to be one of the sexiest women of all time. He'd always thought the resemblance between them uncanny. "That's a brilliant idea. Mom will love that."

"Glamour or rock 'n' roll. There are a few different ways we could go with 1950s!"

As much as he'd liked the idea of Bailey as Audrey, rock 'n' roll held more appeal when he thought of his family. They weren't really the formal type. And Bailey would look just as sexy in one of those poodle skirts. "Let's go with rock 'n' roll."

She nodded. "Good idea. Rock 'n' roll costumes are easier and less expensive for people. This will be so much fun. You'll have to grow some sideburns, but your leather jacket is pretty much perfect already." Then suddenly her face fell. "Hey, when are Callum and…and Chelsea getting married? We're not going to overshadow their celebrations, are we?"

To be honest, that thought hadn't even entered Quinn's head, but he could only imagine how uncomfortable the prospect of Callum's upcoming nuptials must be for Bailey. She might have been the one to end the relationship, but he'd moved on so fast, and his engagement to the woman Bailey had hired to break up with him for her had surprised them all. "Nope. They've fixed a date for the end of May. He's hoping the restaurant will be finished by then and they can be the distillery's first wedding."

"Guess they won't be asking me to handle that event," Bailey said wryly.

By May, Quinn realized, Bailey's bump would be well and truly showing, and if he had his way, everyone would know the baby was his. "Might be a little awkward," he agreed.

She sighed and Quinn wondered if she regretted losing Callum. It had to be hard for her seeing him (or, at least, hearing about him) being so happy with Chelsea just months after Bailey broke up with him. Part of Quinn wanted to ask and the other part of him didn't want to know the answer. He knew she thought sleeping with him had been one of her less clever moments, but he didn't regret it. He couldn't. Sitting across from her now brought up feelings he'd been trying to ignore for years—since he was a horny teenager and she was his mom's friend's daughter, meaning deflowering her wasn't an option. Not if he wanted to live to see adulthood. Sitting across from her now, he really wanted to sleep with her all over again, which just went to show his lack of scruples—the woman was lying to him by omission, for goodness' sake, and he was here only because of the baby.

"How is the restaurant planning going?" she asked, an obvious attempt to direct the conversation elsewhere.

"Really good. Mac's submitted the plans for building approval and is ready to start as soon as they get the go-ahead. Lachlan's already cooking up a storm creating a new menu."

"Those brothers of yours don't let the grass grow when they get an idea, do they?" Bailey said with an affectionate smile.

Quinn tried to smile back, but it was clear she didn't include him in the same category as his aspirational siblings. No wonder she didn't think him father material. Having no idea how to respond, he was glad when Daphne arrived with their meals.

"Thanks," they said in unison.

"You're welcome. Shout if you need anything else."

As Daphne left again, Quinn picked up one half of his sandwich and took a bite. It was good, but he couldn't fully enjoy it. He glanced across at Bailey and saw that she seemed to be having similar issues. Although she'd torn off a piece of frittata with her fork, she didn't look too keen on the idea of putting it in her mouth.

He nodded toward her plate. The frittata looked and smelled amazing, but she'd turned a little green again. "Is something wrong?"

"No." She shoved the fork in her mouth and looked as if she might gag.

"So," she said when she'd swallowed that mouthful, "1950s rock 'n' roll. Do you want me to talk directly to

Lachlan about the food? See what he can do in keeping with the theme?"

When he nodded, she continued. "Would you like a band or a DJ? I know a group that specializes in music from that era. They are the best, but they might be a little pricey."

"Money isn't an issue. I want this night to be special for Mom. Can you see if this band is available?"

She nodded and jotted down another note. "Do you still want to hire a marquee?"

"Yes, I think so. Pity the new restaurant won't be ready in time."

"I'll also need a guest list for numbers. And we'll need to work out tables and chairs and…" She continued listing off various things.

Quinn's head spun with the decisions to be made, but he didn't want her to think he couldn't even handle a simple birthday party, so he attempted to keep up.

"If you have time, we can head on over to the stationers after lunch and select the invitations, or would you prefer to use the Paperless Post app?" Bailey took another sip of her soda.

"Nah, let's do proper invitations." He continued with his sandwich as she chattered on about other things they needed to decide on. He tried to sound enthusiastic, but he guessed that later he likely wouldn't be able to remember half of the things they'd discussed. His head was too full of baby. Bailey pushed her food around on her plate, but he couldn't help noticing she didn't eat any more. He bit his tongue to stop himself from asking her how bad the morning sickness was and suggesting she try some ginger tea.

As he swallowed the last bite of his sandwich, a

woman with a pram approached their table. It took a second for Quinn to recognize her, as he was so focused on the baby. He guessed it was about six months old and it had thick, dark curls framing its cute, dimpled face.

"Oh, my God," exclaimed the woman. "Bailey Sawyer? Quinn McKinnel?"

Bailey glanced up and her eyes widened in surprise. "Cindy Lemmon! I didn't know you were back in town."

"And I didn't know you and Quinn were together," said the woman, whom he now recognized as a girl who'd been in their year at school. If he remembered rightly, she'd left town to pursue an acting career right after graduation, but he'd never seen her in anything.

"Oh, we're not together." Bailey sounded appalled by the idea. "We're…" While she fumbled to explain their relationship, Quinn held out his arms and smiled at the baby as if it was the most delightful thing in the world. This couldn't have worked out better if he'd planned it.

"That's one gorgeous little baby you got there, Cindy. Can I hold her?"

Bailey felt her eyes goggling when Quinn took hold of the baby as if doing so were the most natural thing in the world. He smiled down at the little girl now sitting in his lap, then made a goofy face and silly noises. The baby giggled in the way that only babies could; Cindy grinned down at the sight and Bailey felt her heart clenching inside her.

"You're so good with her," Cindy said.

Quinn barely looked up as he shrugged one shoulder. "I love babies. I can't wait to be a dad one day."

Bailey almost choked on nothing. Thank God she hadn't just taken a sip of her drink or she would surely have spurted it out all over the table at this announcement. How did fatherhood pair up with his dedicated bachelorhood?

"Since when?" she found herself asking.

He glanced over at her, his expression bemused, as if that was an utterly ridiculous question. But instead of answering it, he hit her with another one. "Don't *you* want to have children?"

"Well, of course I do," she spluttered, which was a darn good thing considering her current predicament. "I just never imagined *you* as the settling-down and starting-a-family type."

Quinn didn't reply; he merely returned his attentions to the cherub in his arms and continued to make silly baby noises. He did look very comfortable with the child. *Just goes to show you don't know everything about me, Bailey Sawyer.* His words of earlier repeated inside her head. She'd always thought of Quinn as an open book, but he'd surprised her twice today. Had she been too quick to think the worst of him?

"Well," Cindy announced, leaning against the stroller and smiling down at the laughing duo, "I reckon you'll make an awesome dad. Pity I can't say the same about Daisy's father."

"Is her dad not around?" Quinn asked, his laughter fading.

Cindy sighed and flicked her long golden hair over her shoulder. "Oh, he gets around alright, but unfortunately a wife and child cramped his style, so he cut us loose. I've moved back home with my parents."

"That sucks." Quinn offered Cindy a sympathetic smile. "I'm sorry, but he's the one missing out."

Cindy blushed a little and actually fluttered her eyelashes. "I know not all men are like him. We'll find Mr. Right one day."

Was she flirting with Quinn? Bailey fought the urge to tell her to back off, that Quinn couldn't take the role of Daisy's pseudo-father because he was going to have a biological child very soon. But it wasn't just the baby. Bailey had to admit, if only to herself, that she didn't like the idea of any other woman getting her claws into Quinn. Her head might not think him Mr. Right, but, after their one night together, her heart and body very much disagreed. This was why, if she wanted to protect her heart, she had to be so very careful around him.

She cleared her throat. "We're actually working right now." She knew she sounded rude, but being so close to Quinn had been hard enough *before* he started bouncing a baby on his knee. "I guess if you're back in town we might see you round."

"Oh, right. I'm sorry." Cindy blinked and reached out to take Daisy.

"We should all catch up sometime," Quinn said. "And if you ever need a babysitter, you know, while you're out on a date or something, I'm your man." He tapped himself on his chest.

"Right. Thanks." Cindy smiled, but it didn't quite reach her eyes. Bailey could tell she'd rather Quinn *be* the date than the babysitter, whereas she would rather he stay clear of Cindy altogether.

They said their goodbyes, and as Cindy pushed the stroller away, Quinn leaned back in his seat. "That was a little rude."

"She was all over you," Bailey blurted, before thinking better of it.

"You're not jealous, are you?" His eyes danced with amusement.

"Of course not," she scoffed, her own cheeks heating. It was the closest they'd come to discussing their night together. Maybe now would be the perfect time to tell him the results of that night. If he could get so excited over an old friend's baby, maybe she'd underestimated how he would feel about his own. About *their* own. Her heart quickened and she opened her mouth, but shut it again immediately.

Would telling him now be for the right reasons? She didn't want to do so because she was jealous of his friendliness to Cindy and her baby. And it was still early days. Wasn't the rule not to tell anyone until the three-month mark? Granted, that probably didn't include the father, but these were extenuating circumstances.

Quinn gestured to her barely touched plate. "Are you going to eat any of that?"

She glanced down at it and her stomach churned at the thought as she pushed it away. "I'm not that hungry." He'd already finished his sandwich and she needed some fresh air to clear her head. "Shall we head on over to the stationers?"

Quinn nodded. "Let's do it." He pushed back his seat, the legs of the chair scraping against the polished cement floor as he stood. She stood as well and tried not to stare as he pulled on his jacket. She contemplated asking him not to wear it anymore in her presence because it only amplified his sex appeal, which was the last thing she needed to be thinking about right now. So much for thinking that spending more time with him would dilute the attraction and tame her lust-crazed, pregnancy-affected hormones.

She swallowed and dug her wallet out of her purse.

"I'm paying," Quinn announced, taking his own wallet from his jacket.

"But you're my client."

He raised one eyebrow and hit her with a look that dared her to continue with this argument. "Yes, and we need to discuss your fees, but as I haven't paid you anything yet, getting the lunch you didn't even eat is the least I can do."

Bailey didn't have the energy to argue and knew that, where Quinn was concerned, it was best to pick her battles. She let him pay and waited by the door as he did so.

"How far is this shop?" he asked a few minutes later.

"Not far at all. We may as well walk."

He nodded and opened the door, holding it as he gestured for her to go through. She stepped past him and almost shrieked when he placed his hand in the small of her back. Her insides heated as if flicked by a match and she bit her lip, praising the Lord he couldn't see the expression on her face. It was stupid to be so affected by a tiny brush of his hand, especially when he didn't mean anything by it, but the problem was her body had a perfect memory. The moment he touched her, it recalled all too clearly the sparks they'd created the last time they were up close and personal, and it wanted an encore performance.

Totally flustered, Bailey walked quickly down the sidewalk, putting as much distance between them as she could. Quinn caught up and chattered casually about the weather—how they were having a particularly cold spell. Funny, right now she didn't feel cold at all, and the last thing she wanted to talk about with him was the weather.

Finally, they arrived at her favorite little stationery

shop. This time Bailey held the door open and made sure Quinn had stepped right inside before she followed. She averted her gaze so as not to be distracted by his delicious behind and then made a beeline to the preprinted invitations along one wall. The sooner they made a decision, the sooner she could escape Quinn's tantalizing company.

"See anything you like?" She pointed to a row of sixtieth birthday invitations. "We can go with a classic sixtieth design or we could choose a fun 1950s one like this instead. We just give the printers the details of the party and they'll have them done up specially." The design in question had a vintage jukebox on the side and the slogan Bop Till You Drop across the top. There were others with milk shakes, poodles and swing skirts, all of which would suit their theme.

Quinn screwed up his face as if he didn't approve of any of them and turned slowly to glance over to the other side of the store at the supplies for creating handmade cards. "I'd prefer something a little bit more unique, more personal. Know what I mean?"

"You want to *make* the invitations yourself?" Once again, Bailey found herself surprised and unable to hide it.

"Well, I was hoping you'd help," he said, winking as he grabbed hold of her hand and pulled her across the room.

Oh, help me, God, she thought as electricity shot from his hand right up her arm. *What on earth has gotten into him?*

He paused in front of rows of card stock, paper punches, ribbons, stickers and a whole host of other cutesy things one could purchase to create a truly unique invitation. Bailey agreed that some of the samples on display were gorgeous, but did Quinn have any idea how much time and effort they'd need to put into making something like that?

He dropped her hand and picked up a tiny yellow rubber ducky. "How adorable is this?"

"Not really the image we're going for," she said while inwardly thinking how perfect it would be for a baby shower party or even a birth announcement. It was almost like Quinn knew, but that was impossible. Despite having eaten next to nothing, her stomach rolled at the thought.

He sighed. "You're probably right. But *those* are perfect." And then he stretched past her in his efforts to grab a handful of tiny black vinyl records, and she caught a whiff of his aftershave, a woodsy, musky scent with a hint of vanilla that had always driven her wild. Even if she'd never allowed herself to admit this.

When he straightened again, he was somehow even closer. So close she could feel his breath against her face. Again, memories she'd been trying to forget were invoked and all she could think about was what he'd tasted like and how his lips had felt against hers. The skin at the back of her knees tingled at the recollection and she squeezed her legs together trying to ignore the sensations that erupted between them.

"What do you think?"

For the life of her she couldn't work out what he was referring to. *Oh, that's right, the invitations.*

Normally she could plan events and choose invitations with her eyes closed, but normally she wasn't working alongside Quinn and harboring the biggest secret of her life.

She swallowed. "The choice is yours. It's your party."

He met her gaze full-on. "But I value your opinion. And I'll need your help. You're the creative one."

She *should* tell him that she didn't have time, that the predesigned invitations would do the job perfectly, but her mouth had a mind of its own. Somehow she found herself agreeing to spend a whole lot more time with him.

Chapter Four

On Wednesday afternoon—the day she'd arranged for Quinn to come around in the evening and work on crafting the party invitations—Bailey skived off work early and came home to have a nap.

The alarm woke her just before 6:00 p.m. and she showered and made herself presentable, having vowed never to be caught in her pajamas by him ever again. She ate a TV dinner of mac 'n' cheese—not the healthiest option, she knew, but she didn't have the energy to clean up after cooking. After dinner, she set out all the craft and paper supplies they'd bought and then paced up and down her living room, trying to ignore the butterflies dancing in her belly. Truthfully, they felt more like birds of prey than butterflies.

The guilt of not telling Quinn about the baby was weighing heavy on her heart. There still hadn't been an answer to her letter in the paper, and deep down she knew this was a decision she needed to make for herself.

The last few days he'd shown her a different side of himself, which only confused her more. It had been much easier hating him when he'd been cold and pushing her away, much easier to justify not telling him about the baby.

The buzzing of her doorbell jolted her from her thoughts and she glanced down at her watch. *He's early.* Her stomach flipped. She was supposed to have thirty more minutes to prepare herself. Taking a deep breath, she pinched her cheeks and ran her fingers through her hair as she headed for the front door. Not bothering to look through the peephole, she pulled back the door and pasted a smile on her face.

"Hi… *Mom?*"

"Expecting someone else?" Marcia Sawyer leaned forward and pecked her on the cheek. "What are you all dressed up for? You going on a date or something?"

"I'm not all dressed up," she countered, now second-guessing her chosen attire of black trousers and a smart pink shirt. "And I'm definitely not going on a date." What did her mom think of her? If she were going on a date, she'd wear something a lot sexier. Not that she'd been on an actual date for eons; Callum had been far too busy working in the last six months—since his dad died—for any such frivolity.

"Pity." Marcia's face fell as she stepped inside. "It's time you put yourself back out there. Lord knows Callum didn't let the grass grow." This was the closest her mom had ever come to a mean word about Bailey's ex-fiancé— the hardworking, responsible eldest McKinnel.

She chose to ignore it. "What can I do for you, Mom?"

"Isn't a mother allowed to check in on her daughter? You've barely seen or talked to me in weeks."

Bailey couldn't deny she'd been keeping a low profile where her family was concerned, but this was especially true when it came to her mother, who had a sixth sense about certain things. She was terrified her mom would take one look at her and know something was up. In one way it would be nice to be able to confide in her about the baby, but the fact she and Quinn's mom were best friends made this impossible. Marcia found keeping secrets hard at the best of times, and Bailey couldn't risk him finding out through the grapevine.

"Sorry, I've been very busy with work. And I'm really trying to get my own event business off the ground. In fact, that's what I'm doing tonight. I have a client coming soon."

"Oh, wonderful," Marcia said, looking past her to the table laden with craft supplies. "Anyone I know?"

Bailey opened her mouth to lie, but her mom would be able to see right through her. Better to stick to the truth, even if not the whole truth.

"Quinn McKinnel." She nodded, working hard to sound normal as she said his name. "You have to *promise* not to say anything to Nora, but he's throwing a surprise party for her birthday."

"Quinn's organizing a party?" Marcia snorted in a most unladylike manner. "I thought he just attended them."

Bailey fought the urge to defend Quinn. He might not be the most dependable person on the planet, but he was the father of her baby nevertheless, and he managed the distillery warehouse, did he not? "That's not a very nice thing to say about your best friend's son."

Marcia shook her head and grinned. "You know I adore Quinn. Who doesn't love him? It's just..." Her voice drifted off, but Bailey knew what her mom was thinking. He seemed to lack the ambition and drive of his siblings, and if his dating record was any indication, the word *commitment* didn't feature in his vocabulary.

"Well, he might just surprise you. He's being very involved and hands-on with the planning of this party. He wants to make it extra special for Nora. He's coming over to help me make the invitations."

"Really?" Her mother still sounded skeptical. "Maybe I should stick around and help you."

On the one hand, this could be a good idea—having her mom in the room would surely douse any crazy notions her body got about Quinn—but there was that sixth sense to worry about.

"Thanks, but we've got this covered. Sorry I've been so snowed under with work. Maybe we can go for lunch or something soon." *Like, in a few months when I've worked out what the hell is going on in my life.* With these words, Bailey placed her hands on her mom's shoulders and swiveled her around to usher her back out.

And then the doorbell buzzed again. Bailey's stomach tumble-turned at the knowledge that this time it likely would be Quinn. She stared at the back of the door.

"Well?" Marcia raised an eyebrow. "Are you going to open it?"

"Oh, right." Bailey stumbled forward, grabbed the door handle and yanked it open to find Quinn standing on the other side, holding flowers and a bottle of wine.

I can't drink wine was her first thought, closely followed by *Flowers and wine? What does this mean?*

"Hello, Quinn," she heard her mom say, suspicion ringing loud and clear in her words. This did not bode well.

"Flowers." Quinn held them out to Bailey, then glanced to Marcia and back again. "To say thank you for taking on Mom's party. And wine because you might need it after a few hours crafting with me."

Her mom laughed and stepped aside to let Quinn in.

"Nice to see you again, Marcia. Did Bailey tell you about the party?" he asked, kissing her mom on the cheek.

She blushed ridiculously and giggled like a schoolgirl. It appeared no woman was immune to his charms, no matter their age or professed opinion. "Yes. She did. I think it's a splendid idea. Nora deserves to be spoiled. She's had a hard year, losing Conall so suddenly."

At the mention of his father, Quinn's smile faded and his eyes flashed to the floor, but he looked up again almost immediately. "She's lucky she has good friends like you." He was all charm and smiles again, and Bailey wondered if she'd imagined his brief show of emotion. Callum had thrown himself into work to deal with the pain of losing his father, but what had Quinn done? Had he talked to anyone about his loss?

Marcia opened her mouth, but before she could launch into some story about some craziness she and Nora had gotten up to in their youth, Bailey grabbed her arm. "Anyway, Mom was just going," she said, tugging her mother toward the front door. "And we'd better get to work before it gets too late."

She gestured into the dining room, indicating for Quinn to head that way. He and her mom exchanged goodbyes, and then Bailey all but shoved her mom out the door before she could say another word. She guessed she'd be hearing from her again first thing in the morning with a warning to watch herself with Quinn.

Too late, Mom, she thought as she turned to face the man in question. *I'm already in over my head.*

Quinn hit her with an enticing smile as he held up the wine bottle. "Shall I get us a couple of glasses?"

She stared at the bottle as if it were poison; tiny beads of perspiration exploded on her forehead. "We're supposed to be working," she stammered.

"Who says we can't have fun while we work?" he countered.

She swallowed. *My doctor.* But right now she would *kill* for a glass. She had to think quickly. "After all the overindulging during Thanksgiving and Christmas I thought it was time for a detox, but feel free to have a drink without me."

He gave her a slow once-over, and as his gaze skimmed her body, her internal temperature sky-rocketed. "You don't look to me like you need to detox at all, but whatever floats your boat. I'm not big on drinking alone, so why not save it for another time." He paused a moment, then added, "Maybe when you have something to celebrate."

Like a baby? squeaked a voice inside her. "Okay, thanks." She feigned nonchalance when, inside, her heart flapped about like a bird on steroids. "I'm just going to go put these flowers in a vase."

Which was actually code for *I'm just going to go into the kitchen and freak out a little about anything and everything.* Being in a café—in a public place—with Quinn had been one thing, but now that they were completely alone, all she could think about was the sex they'd had and his horrible treatment of her following. Oh-so-hot, followed by oh-so-cold.

"Okay. Go for it." He grinned again and sat down at the table. "I'll get started here."

How could he sit there as if nothing had happened between them? It was like he'd blacked out their shared torrid history. Well, he wouldn't be able to ignore it once she told him about the baby.

With that thought, Bailey turned and fled into the kitchen. She located a vase on autopilot, filled it with water and all but dumped the flowers in. When was the last time someone had brought her flowers? Had to have been Callum in the early days of their relationship. And what the heck was Quinn doing bringing her some? Was this some kind of peace offering? She wasn't sure she bought his excuse about them being a thank-you gift. And had she imagined the heat in his eyes when he'd said she didn't need detox?

Her head spun with confusion as she stared at the flowers, like maybe they carried the answers to all her questions.

"You okay in there?" came Quinn's delicious voice.

"Yes," she called back, then grabbed a glass, filled it with water and downed its entire contents. If only she weren't pregnant, she could have something stronger to get her through spending time with Quinn. Then again, if she weren't pregnant, she probably wouldn't be in such a flap about it. She took another deep breath, summoned her most professional smile and went out to join him.

"Right," she said as she came up to the table. "Oh, you've already started."

"Thought I may as well." He shrugged as she looked down at the black card he'd already started cutting in half. The plan was for them to layer a silver foil over the top and then print the information in bold black font on a clear special paper that would sit over the foil. She'd made up an example last night and had already done the printing. Their task was to put it all together and add the tiny records and other decorative pieces they'd bought. "I hope I'm doing it alright."

"You're doing it perfectly." Keeping a safe distance, she pulled out a seat across from him and sat.

"Thanks for giving up an evening to do this with me," Quinn said, looking over at her. He had the most beautiful eyes, but she tried to focus on his words instead.

"It's my pleasure. I want this to be perfect for your mom."

"Thanks to you, it will be. What else is going on in your life right now?"

He asked the question so casually, but Bailey couldn't think of an answer. One word—*pregnant*—rang loud and clear in her head. "Work is pretty busy at the hotel. Although we don't have many functions in the months after Christmas, we're planning for all the spring and summer events."

"Does your boss know about your plans to do some freelance work?"

Bailey nodded, relaxing a little; she could talk about work till the cows came home. "Yes. She thinks there's lots of potential for business in Jewell Rock. Bend is such an established tourist town now, that some people are wanting something a little less chaotic for their special days."

"Callum is hoping that's the case," Quinn said as he carefully sliced another piece of black card in half.

Bailey found herself watching his hands while he worked, remembering how they'd felt on her body. His thumb scraping over her nipple, his tongue sliding down her stomach, his…

"Sorry, you probably don't want me talking about Callum," he said, snapping her out of her erotic fantasy.

She almost asked, "Who?" Her engagement to his brother felt like a lifetime ago. "It's okay. I probably should feel awkward and upset talking about him, but I don't. That was the major problem between us. Neither of us felt enough to care about breaking up. We should have done it long ago. Your brother is a great guy, but he wasn't the one for me and I wasn't the girl for him."

"I'm glad to hear it."

What the heck did that mean? Bailey swallowed. "I'll find the right guy one day, but I'm holding out for something real, something magic. I want a relationship like Mom has, one like your parents had. They were always so sweet together."

"Looks can be deceiving," Quinn said and then cursed as he made a mistake with the blade, cutting the card unevenly for the first time.

"What do you mean?" He couldn't possibly be insinuating that Nora and Conall McKinnel weren't a match made in heaven. You'd have to have been blind not to see the spark between those two, even after over thirty years of marriage, raising seven children and running a successful business.

"Forget it." He shoved his thumb into his mouth.

"Oh, God. Are you hurt?" She instinctively leaned closer and reached out her hand.

He winced and withdrew his thumb. It was a clean cut, but blood dripped steadily out. "I'll probably live, but have you got any bandages?" he asked, with a rueful smile.

She chuckled. "If you didn't want to do the work, you only had to say. Cutting yourself was a little dramatic. Come on." She stood and nodded toward the bathroom. "Let's go get you all fixed up."

Quinn silently cursed as he followed Bailey into her tiny bathroom. He couldn't believe what he'd almost let slip about his parents. For his mom's sake, that was a secret he planned on taking to the grave, and until tonight, he'd never been tempted to confess it to anyone.

"Rinse your hand under some water," she instructed as she bent down to search through the cupboard under her sink, giving him a perfect view of her even more perfect behind.

Good God! He sucked in a breath, immediately forgetting about his parents, and barely even registering the pain throbbing through his thumb.

"Quinn," she said, straightening again a few moments later, with a tiny first aid kit in her hands. "Water!"

"Right." He stepped forward, wrenched on the tap and shoved his bleeding thumb under it. "Anyone ever tell you you're bossy?"

She bit her lip, closed her eyes briefly and then conjured some antiseptic from her little medical kit. "*Please* turn off the water and then dry your hand." She gestured to a white hand towel on the rail. "It's clean."

He kept his hand over the sink. "It won't be if I dry myself on it. You got an old one or something?"

She yanked the towel off the rail. "That would defeat the purpose," she said as she reached out, took hold of his hand, wrapped the towel around it and held on firmly.

Her fingers against his skin were better than any painkillers and she stood so close he could smell the berry-scented shampoo she must use to wash her hair. He breathed in deeply, unable to think of a sweeter, more alluring scent. As she held the towel around his hand, their gazes met and Quinn wanted to kiss her more than anything. His head might harbor a grudge against Bailey, but his body didn't give two hoots if she was keeping secrets from him. Her tongue darted out to lick her lip and he could tell her thoughts were identical to his. No matter how much she might want to resist him, they were two adults crazy attracted to each other and about to become eternally linked through their baby.

Since learning about her pregnancy last Friday, he'd given her so many opportunities to come clean. He'd shown her his love of babies, picked up a rubber ducky thing at the stationery shop, bought her wine—and she hadn't taken the bait. Maybe upping the ante by kissing her was exactly what he needed to do.

As if Bailey could read his mind, her grip loosened on the towel and she stepped back, but Quinn wrapped his good hand around hers and yanked her close against him before she could retreat. The tube of antiseptic cream slipped from her grasp as her breasts pressed against his chest and her eyes widened. But he knew desire when he saw it, and his was reflected in her eyes. It added fuel to his already burning fire.

He stooped his head and fused his mouth to hers. He meant it to be just a gentle taste of what could be between them, but the moment their lips touched, memories of their one night of heated passion ambushed him. They were right back there in the deserted warehouse, Bailey perched on a whiskey barrel, her legs wrapped around him as he thrust into her. His head buried between her naked breasts. Nothing had ever been more erotic, and in the urgency of coming together, neither of them had given a thought to the possibility of someone stumbling upon them.

It was an image he'd been trying (and failing) to get out of his head since.

After the event he'd wondered if the illicit nature of the act had heightened the experience, but if the way his body reacted to the taste of her lips now was any indication, that wasn't the case. And the best thing was, she kissed him back. As he moved his hands to cup her face, as his tongue deepened the kiss, taking everything from her, she snaked her hands around his back and gripped him as if she never wanted to let go. Her breathing quickened and it was the most beautiful sound in the world. *This* was the most beautiful thing in the world.

He'd kissed his fair share of girls in his time, but those kisses felt like pale imitations when he compared them to this. This felt real and the intensity of his feelings surprised him.

He wanted to claim this woman. He wanted to brand her!

Then Bailey moved her hands around the front and he grinned as he anticipated her ripping his T-shirt up and over his head. The invitations could wait—he'd only suggested handcrafting them so he could spend more time with her, anyway—getting naked trumped everything.

But, instead, she tore her lips from his as she palmed her hands against his chest and pushed hard. He stumbled back and bumped into the hard corner of the vanity.

"What the hell was that?" she asked, wiping her mouth with the back of her hand in apparent distaste. Yet, although she sounded pissed, he got the feeling she was more annoyed at herself than at him. The flush in her cheeks and the way she didn't meet his gaze told him everything he needed to know.

He shrugged sheepishly. "I think in America we call it a kiss, but the French say *un baiser* and the Italians *bacio.*"

She blinked, obviously flummoxed by his response. He resisted the urge to step forward and kiss her again. "I *meant*…why were you doing it to *me*?"

He thought carefully about his answer. There were a number of possible responses, but not all would elicit the reaction he wanted. "I think it's fair to say that although I made the first move, you were very much a willing participant."

She shook her head. "You took me by surprise, that's all."

He raised his eyebrows and took a tentative step toward her. "Methinks the lady protests too much. Look me in the eye and tell me you didn't enjoy that kiss, that you didn't want it as much as I did."

She hesitated a moment and victory danced in his heart.

"What my *body* wants," she said eventually, "is irrelevant. I think we've established there's a certain chemistry between us, but I want more than just chemistry with someone. I want love and commitment."

"Who says I don't?"

She rolled her eyes, made a scoffing noise and wrapped her arms around herself as if she didn't trust them to be free. "What was that you said that night we slept together? And again later when I tried to talk to you about it? Something about just sex. Meant nothing. Yadda, yadda, yadda."

He swallowed. He *had* said that. And that was his

mantra: one hundred percent no-strings-attached red-hot fun. He had his reasons, but a baby shifted his goal-posts. Finding out he was going to be a dad had flicked some internal switch inside him. He'd never felt this passionately about anything before. And luckily his baby-momma was really, really hot.

"Maybe that was how I used to think, but maybe that's just because I hadn't found a woman who made me question that."

She blinked again and then whispered, "What? And now you have? You never looked twice at me until... well, you know."

Hell, yeah, *he knew*, but that wasn't strictly true. He'd noticed her in high school, but he'd also respected her. "Correct me if I'm wrong, but you were engaged to my brother. I wasn't *supposed* to notice you. But try as I have, I can't get you out of my head." Truth—he'd been harboring illicit fantasies about her prior to the baby discovery, but since then he'd found it impossible to think about anything or *anyone* else.

Bailey's hand rushed to her head and she rubbed at a spot on her forehead. "Was the party a ruse, then?"

"Yes and no." He paused. "I do think Mom deserves a celebration, but I also thought maybe if we spent a little time together, you might forgive me for acting like such a jerk. Maybe we could get to know each other better and explore this thing that isn't going away between us."

His heart froze waiting for her to say something. Her body hadn't been able to hide her reaction to his kiss, but how would her head react to his confession? Would she finally give him hers?

Chapter Five

The evening was not progressing at all how Bailey had imagined. They were supposed to be surrounded by paper and glue, and instead she was in the confined space of her bathroom with all six feet of Quinn in such close proximity she could barely breathe. And with her lips still tingling from his kiss, she couldn't think straight, either.

He wanted her? He *wanted* her. He wanted *her*!

It was almost too good to believe, because her heart definitely wanted him, and in an ideal world there was nothing better for a baby than two parents who loved each other. But wasn't that jumping the gun a little bit? He hadn't mentioned love, and even if he wanted to give commitment a shot, did she really want to be his guinea pig? The stakes were higher now. If a relationship didn't work out, then things would be even more awkward between them than they were now, making things even worse for their baby.

"You're right. I do have feelings for you," she admitted. "Physical and emotional ones, but it's all so complicated."

His expression, which had been serious for all of five seconds, lightened again, and like a predator, he closed the gap between them and took hold of her hand with his good one. He brought it up between them, gently kissed her knuckles and whispered, "It doesn't have to be."

Oh, Lord. Her toes curled in her shoes. How much did she want to believe that? But the truth was, he couldn't make that call when he didn't have all the facts. It was on the tip of her tongue to tell him, but once again, something held her back. Right now, with him touching her, she wasn't in the right frame of mind to make such a massive decision.

"It hasn't even been three months since I broke up with your brother," she said instead.

Quinn raised one of his lovely thick eyebrows—she'd never thought of eyebrows as sexy before, but there wasn't one bit of him that didn't ooze appeal. "And he's moved on already. Why shouldn't you?"

Oh, I've well and truly moved on.

"Please, Quinn." She swallowed and extracted her hand from his. "I need some time. To think. Could we finish the invitations another time?"

"Okay." He heaved a sigh and stepped back. She could see the hurt, the disappointment, in his eyes. Quinn McKinnel wasn't used to hearing the word *no* or even *wait* when it came to women, but if, because of her delay, he lost interest, at least she'd know he hadn't been serious about her in the first place.

He turned and strode out of the bathroom. As his boots echoed on her tiled floor, she realized she hadn't tended properly to his hand, but he seemed to have forgotten about that. Part of her wanted to run after him, go all cavewoman and drag *him* to *her* bed.

Just one more night of magic before the baby news changed everything, but she summoned every ounce of self-control she possessed and waited in the bathroom until she heard her front door click behind him. When she finally ventured out, his unique scent still lingered in the air. What would it be like to come home to that alluring aroma everyday? To have it permeate her living space and all her possessions on a permanent basis. Could she dare to believe that a possibility? Or would Quinn—the epitome of footloose and fancy-free—tire of her once the novelty had worn off, like her father had tired of her mother?

That thought killed her desire and she pressed a hand against her belly. Why couldn't things be different? She'd always wanted to be a mother, but her fantasy had been light-years from her reality. In her fantasy she'd had a loving partner to share in the excitement.

A yawn overcame her and she glanced over at the mess on the table. Tidying up could wait until the morning. With sloth-like speed, she checked that the front door had locked behind Quinn and then went through the routine of getting herself ready for bed.

Over the last month or so, her bed had become her refuge and the place she spent pretty much every moment of her spare time. But tonight when she fell into bed, she tossed and turned, and sleep evaded her. She watched the digital alarm clock on the bedside table tick through the hours, and when it buzzed at 7:00 a.m., she leaped out of bed, joyous at the prospect of something that would take her outside of her own head.

After a breakfast of dry crackers and club soda—she

was very much looking forward to the second trimester when she might be able to stomach something else in the morning—she showered and dressed for work. She was halfway to Bend when she pulled her car over to the side of the road. She barely noticed the horn of the car behind, angered by her sudden braking.

Her head fell against the steering wheel and her own horn honked its disapproval.

What the heck was she waiting for? A visual sign from the heavens? A letter from Aunt Bossy telling her what she already knew? That whatever *her* feelings were toward Quinn, however awkward things might be with his family, whether she worried about his fathering capabilities or not, it wasn't her call to make. He was her baby's father and he deserved to know. He deserved to be involved in whatever capacity he wanted to be. It wasn't her right to stop him.

On speakerphone she dialed her boss, claiming a family emergency that meant she'd be late to work. This *was* a family emergency, and in her current state she wouldn't be much use at the hotel, anyway.

Unable to sleep, Quinn had come into the warehouse early, put some music on loud and started working. He was glad he didn't have a job that confined him to a desk, because he needed some hard manual labor to help release the tension building up inside him. Moving barrels should do the trick; even though the distillery's forklift did the heavy part of the lifting, this task was still more physical than taking inventory of already bottled stock. There was also a strange kind of satisfaction in seeing barrels finally leave their position on the storage rack and be taken to their bottling facility. McKinnel's was one of the few boutique distilleries that bottled their own alcohol—something all of them were proud of.

Years ago, when his dad and uncle had first started the distillery, they'd rotated the barrels during the aging process, which took up to two years. Their warehouse was configured with rows of storage, four barrels high. The temperature on each level varied throughout the year, with the top level always being warmer than the bottom.

Along with the type of wood the barrels were made of, the temperature surrounding them greatly affected the flavor of the final product, so traditionally rotation occurred to give each barrel equal time on each level. These days, instead of rotating, they mixed the contents of barrels from different levels together before they bottled the whiskey, and this had the same result as rotation with a lot less labor.

As he climbed up into the forklift, he was glad that this task didn't require a great deal of thought because he had a one-track mind right now. All roads led to Bailey. Walking away from her last night had been the hardest thing he'd ever had to do. It had taken a hell of a lot of willpower not to give in to the urge to tell her he knew about the baby and that they were doing this parenting gig together.

If she'd objected, he'd have kissed some sense into her.

But the vulnerability in her eyes had rivaled the desire and he'd summoned two things he didn't have much of—restraint and patience. Had that been a mistake? His hands gripping the controls tightly, he maneuvered the forklift around a corner faster than he normally would and watched as the barrel he was shifting tumbled onto the hard cement floor. The noise was deafening but nothing compared to the mess of broken wood and spilled bourbon. Barrels didn't always bounce when dropped from a height. *Dammit.*

Of course, Dale, a junior who worked across all distillery areas, chose that moment to whistle into the warehouse. He stopped as he came upon Quinn climbing down from the forklift. Dale glanced at the mess, then offered him a wry grin. "I'd say bad day, but it's barely started."

"And your first job can be cleaning up this mess," Quinn growled as he stalked off in the direction of his office. He was usually a fair and honest guy, and making Dale do his dirty work wasn't fair at all. It wasn't too long ago, when his dad was still alive, that he'd been treated by his brothers as not much more than a junior, himself. He'd apologize to Dale later, but first he needed to get something off his chest.

He sat down at his computer and opened a blank document. He'd never written an Aunt Bossy letter at the distillery before, but this one couldn't wait a moment longer. He needed to get it off his chest.

Dear Pregnant with Mr. Wrong

What next? This letter should be easy to write. What advice could he possibly offer except to tell the writer that she should give Mr. Wrong the chance to step up. To prove his worth. That she owed this not only to the father, but also to the unborn child. His thoughts snapped to the words in her letter—the words he'd read so many times in the last few days that he could recite them like a memory verse. *I'm worried about him being an unsettling influence in my baby's life.*

He thought of how his father's actions had shaped him into the man he was today. He never wanted to be like him, so until now, he'd avoided the possibility of ever getting close enough to a person to hurt them. Or to be hurt. But what if he was too damaged to be a good dad?

He'd watched how much time and dedication Lachlan put into his kids, and while he wanted to do that, he was scared that somehow he'd stuff it up. He wanted to be a father like Lachlan, but what if he messed up? Maybe Bailey was right and their kid would be better off without him in its life.

Fear coiled like a poisonous snake in his gut, but then another emotion overruled it. The absolute desire to be a better man than his father, to be a better man than he had been before now.

"I'm sorry, Bailey," he muttered to himself as he stared down at the weathered piece of paper he'd been carrying around in his pocket since last Friday night. "But you don't get to make that choice."

To hell with it if she found out about Aunt Bossy— there were more important things than his anonymity, and it was time to confront her with what he knew. He stuffed the paper back in his jacket pocket and closed the document without saving it. As he shoved back his office chair to stand, he sensed someone in his doorway. He looked up and felt his heart crash against his chest cavity.

Bailey.

Had she heard him talking to himself? He couldn't speak. He simply stared as she took a step into the office and closed the door behind her.

"Dale said I could find you in your office." She glanced around, taking in her surroundings. "I didn't even know you had an office."

Annoyance flared inside him. No one had any clue how big a role he played here at McKinnel's. Simply because he wasn't in charge of the distilling process like Blair, his name wasn't on a gold plaque in the main building like Callum's and he wasn't the smiley front of the tasting room like Sophie, everyone thought his job a joke. He pushed the anger aside, because his job description wasn't important right now.

He gestured to the chair on the other side of his desk. "Would you like to sit?"

Bailey bit her lip, then nodded. She removed her pale pink winter coat, hung it over the back of the seat and lowered herself down. But she didn't relax. She perched on the edge of the chair as if ready to make a run for it at any moment. He waited in anticipation, because what other reason could she have for seeking him out at work first thing in the morning?

When time dragged and she still didn't speak, he said, "Normally we offer visitors whiskey, but as it's a bit early for that, I could make you a coffee."

She shook her head. "No. I'm okay and I couldn't drink whiskey anyway, because…well…the truth is…" She drew in a deep breath and he thought maybe the whole world had stopped as he waited for her to continue. "I'm pregnant. I panicked when you kissed me last night because I've been trying to work out how to tell you."

He felt a physical jolt to hear the truth tumble from her lips. Until she'd told him, there was always the slight possibility that he'd been wrong about the writer of the letter. Bizarrely, emotion caught in his throat and his eyes watered.

"It's mine?" He had to ask, just to be sure. Part of him hoped she'd tell him no and let him off the hook, but of course, she wouldn't be here if he wasn't.

She nodded and laughed, but it wasn't a funny ha-ha kind of laugh. "You must have really good swimmers."

"But we used a condom," he said, not because it mattered, but more because it was something he thought he would have mentioned if this was the first he'd heard of the pregnancy.

Bailey shrugged one shoulder. "Apparently they are only ninety-eight percent effective. Look, I know this is a shock, a surprise and the last thing we planned, so I want you to know that if you don't want to be involved, I'll understand. We can—"

He cut her off. "How long have you known?"

The way she couldn't meet his eyes told him what he already knew.

"Why did you take so long to tell me?"

She rubbed her lips together and glanced down at the desk, refusing to meet his gaze. "I was scared. And worried—about what everyone would think. As you pointed out when I went to talk to you after Thanksgiving, there's bound to be backlash from our families, even if Callum and I are no longer together. I needed to get my head around it before that."

And he also knew the truth—she didn't know if she could rely on him to be what she and the baby needed. That cut deeper than anything else, and he found he wanted more than anything to prove to her that she was wrong. That she *and* their baby could depend on him.

Quinn pushed back his chair again, and this time he did stand. He walked around his desk and dropped to his knees in front of Bailey. He reached up, cupped her cheek in his hand and turned her head so he could look right into her gorgeous green eyes. For a second, he lost himself in their beauty and forgot what he was going to say. But he pulled himself together.

"This isn't a time to be scared or unhappy or worried about what anyone but you and I think. This is a time to celebrate, to enjoy, and from now on, we're in this together. Okay?"

When she didn't reply, he sliced open his heart. "I know what everyone thinks of me—that the only thing I'm good at is partying and having fun, but I promise you, they don't know the real me. I meant what I said last night about wanting to be with you, and a baby doesn't change that."

Instead, a baby justified their combustible sexual attraction.

A tear slid down Bailey's cheek and Quinn brushed it away with his thumb, then he wrapped his arms around her and pulled her close. She fit perfectly and a sense of rightness came over him. He could have played this differently—when she'd confessed, he could have told her that he already knew, but what good would that do? It would be as useless as holding on to the anger he'd felt when he first read her letter. She'd told him now, and for the first time in his life, he felt like there was meaning and purpose to his existence. Being a father, trying to make a go of things with Bailey, still scared the hell out of him, but he also wanted to succeed at both more than he'd ever wanted to succeed at anything before.

"Are you really okay with this?" came her whispered question a few moments later.

He pulled back, looked her in the eye and hoped his voice didn't quiver as he said, "I'm more than okay."

She let out a half laugh. "You're full of surprises, Quinn McKinnel."

He leaned down to kiss her. As their kiss deepened, Quinn's body hardened in desire, but just as things began to heat up, Bailey pulled away. He tried not to show his frustration as he questioned her with his eyes.

A coy smile twisted her lips as she pressed her hand to his chest. But unlike last night, her touch wasn't a warning. She licked her lips, and man, if it wasn't the most seductive thing he'd ever seen. His appetite for her raged.

"I'm glad you're happy about this," she whispered, "but I don't think we should rush too fast into a relationship. There's more than just our hearts at risk here now. Can we just take things slowly and see where they lead?'

Slow? The word wasn't in his vocabulary—he doubted if it was in any of the McKinnels'—but, as much as his hormones hated him for it, he agreed. "Whatever you want." He wanted Bailey to be comfortable, as any stress on her might transfer to their baby.

"And I think we should also keep the pregnancy between us, for now," she added. "At least until I've had the first scan and know everything is okay."

Quinn agreed that this made sense, especially due to their complicated family situation. "When is the first scan?"

"In two weeks. Do you want to come?"

He raised his eyebrows at her. "What part of 'in this together' didn't you understand? Of course I'm coming!"

Chapter Six

"Bailey?" The hotel receptionist buzzed her desk.

She swallowed the water she'd just sipped. "Yes?"

"I've got a Quinn McKinnel here to see you. Shall I send him in?"

She frowned and looked at her cell to check the time. Was she late to their first ultrasound? Unable to think about anything else all day, it seemed unlikely, but she'd discovered pregnancy brain was a thing, so nothing was impossible. "Sure. Send him through."

She stood to wait for him. Thankfully her boss was out showing a newly engaged couple what the hotel could offer for their upcoming nuptials, so when Quinn strode into the room and kissed her on the lips, there were no witnesses.

"What are you doing here?" she asked, trying to recover from the assault to her senses that was his hot, delicious mouth. "I thought we agreed to meet there."

"I wanted to drive you."

She placed a hand on her belly—there was already a bump, so she'd had to take to wearing baggier clothes than she normally did—and shook her head. "I'm not riding on the back of your bike." As much as the idea of being pressed tightly up against Quinn, her arms wrapped around his torso, appealed, motorbikes were dangerous and she wouldn't risk her baby.

"I wouldn't let you," he whispered. "Not in your condition. Now, are you ready to go?"

Assuming he must have borrowed his mom's car or something, Bailey nodded.

As she turned to pluck her purse and water bottle from her desk, Quinn grabbed her coat. He held it out to her and she slid her arms into the sleeves, then he spun her round and did up her buttons, one by one, like she was a little girl. But standing this close to Quinn, his fingers brushing against her body in his efforts, didn't make her *feel* like a little girl. When he was done, he smiled down at her and something low in her belly quivered. It was too soon for it to be the baby.

They walked out of her office and out of the hotel, careful to keep a distance between them. Then Quinn led her over to a brand-new navy blue SUV parked in the hotel lot. He aimed his key fob and the lights flashed as it unlocked. She paused as he opened the front passenger door.

"What are you waiting for?" he asked, looking back at her.

"Whose car is that?"

A grin spread across his face. "I didn't steal it, if that's what you mean. It's mine. You like it?"

"What happened to the bike?"

He shrugged. "I decided I needed a more family-friendly vehicle. I can't put a car seat on the back of a motorbike, now, can I?"

And just like that, she burst into tears. Quinn McKinnel on his motorbike had always been a welcome sight, but the image of him holding their baby as he gently eased it into its car seat undid her.

"Hey." He stepped toward her and she forgot about the possibility of being seen as he pulled her close. "Is it the color? Whatever you don't like, we can change it."

She sniffed. And then laughed. "It's perfect. It's just…"

"You didn't think I was responsible enough to put baby before bike."

"I was *going* to say my tears were just pregnancy hormones." But he'd nailed it, really. Selling his beloved motorbike was a massive step for him, a true sign of the commitment he said he had for her and their baby. In the two weeks since she'd told him, everything he'd done had reassured her that telling him had been the right decision. He was like a new man.

As he drove through the streets of Bend from the hotel to the clinic, she sipped more water.

"You thirsty?"

"No! I have to drink for the ultrasound and I really, really need to pee, so let's not talk about it."

Quinn laughed, which made Bailey smile despite the discomfort of her full bladder.

"It's not funny."

"Sorry." He didn't sound it and so she punched him in the arm.

"We should talk about something else," he said. "What about baby names? Any favorites?"

Bailey sighed. "I want it to be perfect, but how do you

choose a name for a baby until you've actually seen what it looks like?" It was so surreal to be having this discussion, let alone with Quinn.

"I guess we just write a short list, and then we can make the final decision when the baby's born. I've downloaded a baby name app on my phone. I'll show you when we're waiting, but so far my favorite is McKinley. It works for a boy or a girl."

"McKinley McKinnel?" She snorted and almost wet her pants. "You can't be serious."

He turned his head briefly and hit her with his mischievous grin, the one he'd used on female teachers at school to get out of trouble. "So you're happy for the baby to have my name?"

It was bizarre to realize she'd never actually thought about this; she'd just assumed a baby took its father's name, but if things between them didn't work out, that would mean she'd have a different name than her child. "I guess it's something we need to think about. We could always go double-barreled—like Sawyer-McKinnel or McKinnel-Sawyer."

"Not a fan, myself," Quinn said, his eyes trained on the road. "I always wonder what happens when two people with double-barreled names have kids. Do their children have four surnames? But Bailey McKinnel has a nice ring to it."

Her heart hitched a beat and she almost choked on the water she'd just swallowed. "If that's a proposal, Quinn McKinnel, you'll have to do a lot better. Besides, we're supposed to be taking things slow, remember?" And she wouldn't marry him unless she was one hundred percent certain they were doing it for the right reasons.

He let out a deep sigh as he turned into the clinic parking lot. "I remember."

And he had been on his best behavior these last two weeks. They'd spent a lot of time together, finishing the invitations and making further plans for Nora's party, but kissing had been as far as they'd gone. Quinn had made it clear he would take her lead, but Bailey found herself questioning why she'd insisted on getting to know each other better first. Her head was guarding her heart from getting hurt, but her body didn't care about that kind of pain.

Without another word, he parked his new SUV, then climbed out and went around to hold the passenger door open for her. He didn't take her hand as they walked toward the building, and she told herself this was because he knew she was worried about them being seen, but she felt the loss immensely.

Inside the clinic, Quinn took a seat while Bailey went to check in at the reception desk.

"They're on time," Bailey told him when she returned and lowered herself into the seat beside him. "It shouldn't be long."

"Here's the app I mentioned," Quinn said, angling the screen on his phone for her to see. "You put in the gender, then you can select from a whole host of other categories and they offer you a selection of names."

"Do you want to find out the baby's sex?" she asked, leaning close as she read down the list of categories—letter, religion, nationality, celebrity, traditional, etc.

He deliberated a moment. "You know, I'm not sure I do. What do you think?"

"Another thing I can't decide."

He chuckled and squeezed her hand, just as a tall

woman appeared. "Bailey Sawyer," she called into the waiting room.

"That's us. Well, you," Quinn said as he stood and pulled her to her feet.

As they followed the woman down a short corridor, Bailey swallowed—the squirminess in her stomach like no nerves she'd ever had before.

"You okay?" Quinn whispered, as if he could sense her anxiety.

She blinked and nodded, so glad that she'd made the decision to tell him. He'd been there at conception, so it was right he was here for this next milestone and she couldn't imagine doing this alone. What if there was something wrong with her baby? She couldn't bear thinking about it.

As the sonographer closed the door to the little room behind them, she introduced herself as Sherry and shook both their hands. "Right, Bailey, hop up there for me," she said with a smile as she gestured to an examination table with the back elevated. "Dad, you can take the chair alongside."

The two of them did as they were told and Bailey wondered what Quinn thought of being called Dad. She guessed it was something both of them needed to get used to.

Sherry explained the process of the ultrasound and asked Bailey to pull up her shirt. Although Quinn had seen a lot more of her naked only a few months ago, her cheeks turned pinker as she did so. Then Sherry squeezed a gel—a little cold, she apologized—against Bailey's belly and began to rub it all over with the probe.

"How far along did you think you were?"

"About ten weeks? Why?"

"It's just…your bump is quite big for your dates."

Bailey's heart leaped to her throat at the possibility she'd made a mistake and that somehow the baby was Callum's, not Quinn's. *Please, God, no.* Not only would that be awfully complicated, it would break her heart. This pregnancy might have been unexpected, but she didn't want to parent with anyone but Quinn. She dared a look at him; he'd gone pale, but his face was trained on the screen, which she suddenly realized had an image on it.

"And there's your reason," Sherry announced, her smile coming through in her voice. "Twins!"

"What?" Bailey stared at the image on the screen as it started to take shape in front of her.

"There is a history of twins on my side," Quinn said proudly. "You know my dad was a twin, right? And there's also Lachlan's kids."

"These little babies have nothing to do with heredity," Sherry said. "You're having identical twins and they're a spontaneous event. A miracle, really."

"Identical?" Bailey breathed. "Can you tell the sex yet?"

"I'm sorry. It's too early, but let's have a proper look and check everything is progressing as it should."

Bailey felt Quinn's hand envelop hers and they exchanged a look of wonder before she turned her eyes back to the screen. Their babies looked like two little gray blobs floating in darkness, but they were the most beautiful blobs she'd ever seen.

"I don't want to alarm you," Sherry said, jolting Bailey from her bubble, "but as your babies are sharing the same placenta, there is the slight chance of twin-to-twin transfusion syndrome."

"What's that?" Quinn sounded as alarmed as Bailey felt.

"I'll give you a brochure and your obstetrician will be able to answer any questions you have, but basically it occurs when the twins share an unequal supply of the placenta's blood, which results in the fetuses growing at different rates."

"Is it dangerous?" she and Quinn asked at the same time.

"It can be, but only ten to twenty percent of identical twin pregnancies are affected, so there's more chance of this being a perfectly healthy twin pregnancy than not. Everything certainly looks as it should at the moment, but we'll need to monitor the situation with frequent ultrasounds to make sure things stay that way."

"Okay. Good." Bailey relaxed a little and looked to Quinn, who looked part excited, part terrified.

"I'll print you off some photos," Sherry said, pressing a button on her machine and then tearing off some paper towels from a dispenser. "You can wipe your stomach clean again now, and if you want to use a bathroom, there's one on your left just outside the door."

While Bailey sneaked off to relieve herself, Quinn waited for their ultrasound photos. *Identical twins!* He could hardly believe it as he stared down at the black-and-white images in his hand. He'd barely just adjusted to the idea of *one* baby. It didn't seem two minutes since his brother Lachlan had shown them similar images of his twins, although it was actually almost nine years and technology had advanced a lot since. These photos were much clearer.

As the paper quivered in his fingers, he realized his

hands were shaking—overwhelmed by the news of twins. One baby was terrifying enough, but two! He didn't want to alarm Bailey, but even before Sherry had mentioned the small possibility of twin-to-twin transfusion syndrome, he'd come out in a cold sweat. He knew cerebral palsy like his nephew had wasn't a familial thing, but he also knew that statistically more could go wrong with multiple births. Premature delivery happened frequently with twins and often led to complications.

Twins were double the excitement and double the stress.

Yet seeing the image on the screen had made everything real—his heart had been thumping so hard he thought it might crash, but there'd also been this joy like nothing he'd ever felt before. The thought of anything happening to either of those tiny beings made him feel physically ill. He realized he would do everything within his power, and then some, to protect them. There was so much to do in the next few months to get ready for the biggest adventure of their lives.

"Hey!" The door of the bathroom opened and Bailey emerged. She all but snatched the photos from his grasp. "Oh, my goodness. Can you believe this?"

The pure delight in her eyes and her voice made him smile and he told himself to stop thinking about the worst that could happen and try to enjoy the ride. "Pretty amazing, hey?"

Her smile was so wide he wasn't sure anything could ever wipe it off.

"Do you need to go back to work this afternoon?" he asked.

She sighed and some stray hairs that had fallen across her face flicked up as she did so. "I'm supposed to, but after this—" She waved the photos in front of his face, still grinning. "I'm really not in the right headspace."

"Me, neither," he said. "It's Friday afternoon. Why don't we knock off early? We can go pick up your car, then head back to my place and hang out. I'll make you dinner."

She looked up from the photos a moment. "You cook?"

"Not as well as Lachlan or Mom, but better than the rest of my family." And he figured showing off his prowess in the kitchen could only help his quest to prove what a good parent he could be.

Her eyes sparkled. "This I have to see."

Ten minutes later, Quinn dropped Bailey off at the hotel and she promised to follow as soon as she could. On his way back to Jewell Rock, he popped into the supermarket and picked up all the ingredients he needed to make a creamy chicken-and-veg pasta. It might not sound fancy, but the moment she put the first forkful into her mouth, she'd be begging him to make it again and again. That's if the morning sickness didn't stop her enjoying it. Why did they call it morning sickness, when obviously— if Bailey's experience was any indication—the nausea struck at all hours of the day? With this thought, he added a couple of bottles of ginger ale and some dry crackers to his shopping cart and then headed for the registers.

He and Bailey arrived at his place—a small house he'd got cheap because it was in need of a lot of TLC— at the same time. Until now, they'd been spending their time together at her apartment under the ruse of party planning. Her coming here felt like another step in the right direction.

"You were quick," he said as they climbed out of their respective vehicles.

"My boss had already gone home, so I didn't have to make any excuses." She was still clutching the little strip of photos like they were the winning ticket to tonight's lottery super draw, but as she approached him, she glanced at her car.

"Relax," he said, grabbing his grocery bags out of the trunk, "if anyone sees your car, they'll just assume you're here working on Mom's party." The invitations had gone out last week.

She raised one eyebrow. "And if your mom sees?"

"*That* is a good point." He sighed as he shut the trunk. "And something we need to discuss. Now we've had the scan and the babies look healthy, we should decide how and when to tell the world our news. You're already starting to show and it won't be too long before you won't be able to hide behind baggy clothing."

Some of the pleasure that had been on her face dimmed at these words, but she nodded nonetheless. He knew she was scared about what people might think, but he figured it was a bit like ripping off a bandage. The sooner they did it, the sooner they could deal with any fallout.

"Come on. Let's go inside out of the cold."

"I'm glad our babies will be born late summer," she said as she followed him up the garden path. "At least I won't have to get up in the middle of the night in the freezing cold."

Something squeezed inside Quinn at the way she referred to herself—as if she'd be the one getting up with the babies and doing all the tough parenting stuff. As if, despite his being there, she didn't really believe he'd stick it out. Telling their families wasn't the only thing they needed to work out.

He unlocked his house and pushed open the front door.

"Why don't you go lie on the couch while I put away these groceries and make us a drink?" he suggested as they stepped inside.

Bailey groaned. "I'd kill for a coffee, but…" She gestured to her stomach, still hidden by her coat. He swallowed as he remembered the glimpse he'd gotten of bare skin that afternoon.

"You know," he said, trying to turn his thoughts from X-rated to PG, "I've been reading a bit about pregnancy, and research says that you *can* have coffee, you should just limit it to one or two cups a day."

"Really?"

He nodded. "How about you treat yourself in celebration of our twin news?"

She grinned at him as she clutched the photos to her chest. "You've twisted my arm."

"I can be very convincing when I want to be."

Quinn went into the kitchen to unpack the shopping and brew the coffee, and Bailey went to put her feet up. He joined her five minutes later, carrying two steaming mugs, to find her flicking through one of the pregnancy books he'd ordered on the internet. A confirmed bachelor, he didn't usually invite women back to his place, so it was weird to see her looking so comfortable on his couch. But he didn't freak or break out in a cold sweat, so that was a start.

She glanced up. "When you said you'd been doing some reading, you weren't overexaggerating. You were quick to get these."

He merely smiled as he put their drinks down on the coffee table, then he sat down beside her and put his arm around her shoulders. "I like to be well-informed. And books are my friends."

"So I see," she said, looking past the pile of pregnancy books to the shelves beyond that were bursting with literature in many different genres. "I didn't know you were a big reader."

"I wasn't really at school. Kinda got into it later on. Contrary to popular belief, there's more to me than good looks and charm." He leaned forward, picked up a mug and held it out to her.

"Thanks." She smiled at him as she wrapped her fingers around it and then closed her eyes and moaned when she took a sip. "*Oh. My. God.* You don't know how good that tastes after almost two months of going without."

Watching her expression of ecstasy, Quinn thought he had some kind of idea. Or at least he could imagine. He reckoned he might make a similar noise of satisfaction when they finally slept together again. Muscles tightened all over his body and he tried to think of something besides sex, something that would kill the erection now rising in his jeans.

"When do you think we should tell our families about us? And about the twins?"

She turned her face to him and screwed up her nose. "Can't we just run away somewhere?"

"I'm down with that idea. Why don't we go to Vegas and elope? Then we could embark on a round-the-world trip and return home in autumn with two kids in tow." He was only half kidding, but it turned her scowl into a smile.

She laughed. "If only. My mom would never forgive me. Not only for the elopement, but also for not letting her be there when her first grandchildren are born." Her smile suddenly faded. "I'm sorry. I just realized how tough this must be for you, about to become a dad without your father around. You must miss him terribly."

"Of course." Quinn tried to keep his expression neutral. He didn't care that his father wouldn't meet his children; if anything, he was glad his old man wouldn't have the chance to lie and pretend to them, as well. "Let me have a look at those photos again."

She picked them up and passed them to him "Do you want them to be girls or boys?"

"I don't care," he said, in awe of the black-and-white images in his hands. "As long as they're healthy."

"Neither do I." She took another sip of her coffee. His mind, still thinking about his dad, despite the fact he'd rather not, came to linger on her biological father. Her mom had been with Bailey's stepdad for as long as he could remember, and being a guy and not really interested in such stuff, he'd never questioned his mom about Bailey's real father.

"Are you going to tell your dad about the twins?" he asked.

"Well, when we tell Mom and everyone, Reginald will be there."

"I meant your biological father. You've never said much about him. At least not that I've heard. What's the story there?"

He felt her tense beside him. "He married Mom because they were young and pregnant, with me—their families expected them to do the right thing—but my dad wasn't the settling-down type. He broke up with Mom before I was born, then was in and out of my life for about ten years. When Mom met Reginald, I think he was relieved, like it let him off the hook or something. He friended me on Facebook a few years back, but we're not really in contact aside from that. Reginald is my father in all the ways that matter."

It sounded like a rehearsed speech, as if she didn't really care, but Quinn could read between the lines. He could read her body language. Suddenly her reticence to tell him about their baby made even more sense. Her father's apathetic behavior had hurt her badly, and because of this, she feared that maybe Quinn would be like her deadbeat dad.

Like hell he would.

"I'm sorry," he said.

"What for? You're not my father."

He chuckled at that. "Thank God. Then this would be very, *very* wrong." He leaned over and put the photos down on the table, then he turned back and took hold of her hand. "I meant, I'm sorry for taking advantage of you when you were upset about Callum. When you came to me, confused and hurt, I should have listened, but instead I—"

"Instead you distracted me and then made me even more confused." Her hand moved, taking his with it to rest on her tiny bump. "But I'm not sorry. I can't be sorry for this."

Although her jumper stopped him touching her bare belly, this felt as intimate as they'd been since that day in the warehouse. As their eyes met and he breathed in the berry scent that wafted from her hair, Quinn prayed for self-control. He'd promised Bailey they'd take things slowly, but right now—alone in his house, squished together on his couch—his body hated him for taking that vow. He swallowed, wanting to kiss her but unable to trust himself not to take the next logical step.

Then, while he was deliberating and beating himself up, Bailey leaned closer and kissed *him*.

She wasn't gentle, she wasn't reserved. She grabbed on to his shirt, scrunched the material up in her hands and yanked him close. As her tongue slid into his mouth with a ferocity that matched the hunger raging inside of him, she climbed onto his lap so she was straddling him on the couch. The V of her thighs pressed against him; there was no hiding his desire now.

The voice inside his head warning him to take things slow struggled to be heard as Bailey slid her hands into his hair. Her breasts—definitely larger than normal now—pressed against his chest and his hands itched to hold them. Instead, he cupped her face and broke their kiss, searching her eyes. "Are you sure about this?"

"Shut up and undress me."

He wasn't stupid. When a pregnant woman made demands, any guy worth half his salt would give her what she wanted. Feeling like a teen whose first girlfriend had just told him to pop her cherry, he yanked her top up and over her head. Her breasts, practically bursting from a lacy pink bra, bobbed in his line of sight and he worked quick to rid her of that garment, as well.

A guttural moan escaped his mouth as he paused to admire the view. Two of the most delicious breasts in the history of humankind, his to taste, tease and admire. It felt like all his Christmases had come at once.

Bailey laughed. "You're allowed to touch them, you know." Then she took hold of his hands with hers and placed them atop her breasts. His jeans shrank three sizes.

"God!" was all he could manage to say, and then instinct took over.

Chapter Seven

"Wake up, sleeping beauty."

At the sound of Quinn's voice, Bailey opened her eyes. It took a few moments for her to orientate herself, and when she did, *when she remembered*, her lips broke into a smile.

She was naked, thoroughly satiated, in his bed. They were having twins and she'd just had the best sex of her life. He was shirtless, too—thank God for central heating—and sitting on the edge of the bed holding a tray of something that smelled divine. She waited for the usual wave of nausea that hit whenever she smelled pretty much any food these days, but it didn't come. Or maybe they'd just worked up so much of an appetite that the morning sickness had taken a backseat.

"That smells amazing," she said, slowly sitting up and pulling the covers with her. Although he'd seen her without a scrap of clothing and done things to her she'd only ever read about in erotic romances, she wasn't ready to have a normal conversation while naked. "How long have I been asleep?"

"A few hours." He grinned. "But it gave me time to whip up something nutritious. You hungry?"

"Famished." She stared down at what looked to be a bowl of creamy pasta and tried not to drool.

"Do you need to use the bathroom before we eat?" he asked.

Now that she thought about it, she did need to pee—since getting pregnant, she pretty much needed to pee all the time. When she nodded, he put the tray on the bedside table and then grabbed an old T-shirt that was hanging over the end of the bed and offered it to her.

"Thanks." She smiled as she took it and slipped it over her head. The material was soft against her bare skin, but best of all, it smelled of him. She pulled back the covers, climbed out of bed and headed into his bathroom. After relieving herself, she washed her hands and then saw a bottle of his cologne. Unable to resist a quick sniff, she unscrewed the lid and inhaled. The tantalizing aroma, a cocktail of something woodsy mixed with vanilla made her head spin. Vanilla had always been her favorite scent—as a child, whenever her mom baked with it, Bailey had loved holding the bottle under her nose—but the smell of Quinn had just leaped to first place.

Feeling more content than she had in a very long while, she put the bottle back in its place and returned to the bedroom.

He wolf whistled as she emerged. "I could get used to the sight of you barefoot and wearing nothing but my shirts."

The heat in his gaze made her feel like the sexiest woman on the planet and she smiled as she crawled back into bed beside him. "And if this food tastes as good as it smells, then I could get used to your cooking."

In reply, he dug a fork into the bowl of fettuccine, twirled it round and then lifted it to her lips. She opened her mouth and every nerve ending in her body tingled as he slid the fork inside. Her eyes closed of their own accord and her taste buds sighed with contentment as she chewed and swallowed the first mouthful.

"Well?" he asked when she opened her eyes again.

"Give me more."

Quinn laughed and obliged. They ate from the same bowl, talking and stealing the odd kiss along the way.

"Did we make any decisions regarding the announcement of our news?" Bailey asked, the day a little bit of a blur since their twins discovery.

"Nope. You kind of distracted me."

A warmth flushed over her skin at the smile behind his words. "Sorry about that," she said, not feeling or managing to sound apologetic in the slightest.

"*Yeah.* Sure you are. Fancy taking advantage of me like that." He shook his head as he slipped another forkful into her mouth.

When the bowl was scraped clean, Quinn took it back into the kitchen, then returned to the bed and climbed in beside her. He pulled her close against him, and as she sipped the ginger ale he'd bought for her, they talked some more.

"This is going to sound stupid, since I grew up at the distillery almost as much as you did, but although I know you work in the warehouse, I'm not sure exactly what your role is." She hoped he didn't take offense, but she wanted to get to know him better.

"I guess I'm a jack-of-all-trades, master of none." Although he made a joke of it, she detected a hint of hurt in his voice. "Like you said, I grew up with the distillery in my blood. I'm very proud of my heritage, but as the youngest, aside from the twins, everyone had already taken the important jobs by the time I finished school. Callum has always had a head for business, more than our father, it seems, and Blair did his time alongside Dad, learning the craft of distilling. There wasn't room for me, as well.

"I guess I should have gone off and done something else, like Mac, Lachlan and the girls did, but I started helping out in the warehouse after finishing school and I never left. In addition to keeping track of all our stock and overseeing the delivery of orders to all our various clients, I help Blair with the bottling, and occasionally Callum even lets me out to try to woo new clients."

"He never mentioned that."

Quinn snorted. "He wouldn't have. He likes to take all the credit. He's a lot like our father in that respect."

"There's always been a kind of rivalry between you two, hasn't there?"

"Who? Me and Dad?"

"No." She chuckled. "You and Callum."

He shrugged. "Maybe it's because I always wanted what he had. Anyway, let's not talk about him or business. We've got so many better things to focus on."

Bailey couldn't argue with that. She leaned into him and rested her head against his shoulder as they resumed their earlier conversation about names. Choosing one had seemed daunting, but now they needed two.

"Do you want to follow your family's tradition of Scottish names?"

"I never really thought about it, but Quinn is the least Scottish sounding to me and Bailey is quite modern. Both our names could be male or female, so maybe we should go in that direction for the twins' names. I think unisex names are kinda cool and can be used whether we have boys or girls."

"You mean like Avery and Jesse? Morgan and Jules?"

He nodded. "Yes, exactly. And I like those ones. They're going on the list."

If it had felt surreal being in the ultrasound clinic with Quinn, it felt even more surreal snuggling in his bed and chatting about an entwined future. Surreal, but also natural, blissful and right. As if, after a long journey down the wrong road, fate had finally nudged her in the right direction. And now that she'd arrived, she was so comfortable, she never wanted to leave this bed.

But as their names list grew longer and more and more outrageous, the minutes ticked into hours and it started to get late. That postcoital nap had given Bailey a second wind, but she couldn't ignore the exhaustion creeping up on her again. As much as she hated to do so, she started to get up.

Quinn's arms tightened around her. "Where do you think you're going, young lady?"

She smiled at his playful tone. "It's late. I should be getting home."

"Stay." That one word sounded more intoxicating than any of the sweet nothings he'd whispered in the throes of passion.

While a tiny voice inside her head reminded her of the sensible decision she'd made to take things slow, there were a hundred other voices telling her to relax back into his arms. That afternoon she'd slept better in his bed than she had in the last two months; the prospect of a good night's slumber and the possibility of morning wake-up sex won out.

"Okay," she replied as she relished the warmth of his naked skin against her. "You twisted my arm. Again."

"I knew something was going on!"

Quinn woke up on Saturday morning to Bailey in his arms, light sneaking in through a gap in his curtains and his mother standing at the end of his bed, her fists perched on her hips as she glared down at them. As if things couldn't get any worse, Marcia, Bailey's mom, stood beside her, also a vision of feminine fury.

"Oh, my God!" Bailey shrieked, leaping away from him and pulling the covers over her.

"What the hell are you two doing in here?" Quinn demanded, sitting up and trying to shield Bailey from their view.

"I used the spare key to get in," Nora said, her chin jutting upward as if she had nothing to be ashamed about. She looked to her friend and then back to the bed. "We had our suspicions about you two, and then when I went for an early-morning walk this morning, I saw Bailey's car and—"

It was on the tip of Quinn's tongue to ask her who in their right mind goes walking early in the middle of winter. But this was his mom they were talking about and there were other more pressing issues. Like getting the two meddling women out of his bedroom. He pointed to his open door. "And now you can get out again!"

"We're not going." Marcia's eyes narrowed at Quinn as if he were the wolf and her daughter Red Riding Hood.

"Until you tell us what is going on between you two," Nora finished.

"I thought that would be fairly obvious." When neither of their mothers said a word but simply folded their arms and raised their eyebrows in unison, he added, "Fine. At least give us a chance to get dressed. We'll be out in a moment."

With obvious reluctance, their mothers retreated. As the door closed behind them, Quinn turned to Bailey, who looked as if she could burst into tears or throw up at any moment.

"Are you alright?" He reached out to her, but she leaped out of bed and rushed for his bathroom. Seconds later he heard the telltale signs of morning sickness.

He found her kneeling on the floor, stooped over his toilet as she heaved up the contents of last night's dinner.

"There, there," he crooned as he crouched beside her, held her hair out of her eyes and rubbed her naked back. "It'll be okay."

A strangled moan escaped her mouth. A few moments passed, then she looked at him—her eyes wide and accentuated by her long lashes, her cheeks turned a deep crimson. "Are you *crazy*? That is the most embarrassing thing that has ever happened to me. My own mom would have been bad enough, but your mom, as well! I'll never be able to look either of them in the eye again."

Even in her mortified, postsick state, she looked gorgeous and he had a crazy urge to draw her into the shower and have her again. To hell with their moms waiting impatiently on the other side of his bedroom door. Instead, he stroked her hair. "Relax—we're both adults. If anyone is in the wrong here, it is them."

She let out a maniacal giggle. "*So* wrong."

"Come here." He pulled her against him and heaved them both off the cold tiles. "Let's get dressed and go and face the music. Or rather, The Moms."

At these words, Bailey cursed—something she rarely did.

"What is it?" he asked at the terror in her voice.

"My clothes. They're still strewn all over your living room floor."

He swallowed a curse of his own. "You can wear some of my sweatpants, that T-shirt, and I'll find you a sweater." He went to kiss her forehead, to try to calm her, but she shook her head furiously.

"No. You'll have to go and get my own clothes. I can't face them dressed in your gear. *Please?*"

He wanted to reason with her that him going out there alone to collect her clothes from wherever they'd landed was an equally bad idea, but she pushed him toward the door as if it was a done deal. "I'll have a quick shower and freshen up while you're getting them."

Women. Quinn grabbed a pair of jeans and yanked them on, then pulled a clean T-shirt out of his drawer and put that on, too. Hoping the moms might be in the kitchen helping themselves to coffee or something, he opened his door without making a sound and tiptoed out toward the living room. He moved like a burglar in his own place. This was like no walk of shame he'd ever done before and unfortunately he found his mom and hers perched on his couch waiting when he emerged. Between them, in a neat folded pile, were Bailey's clothes. Her bra and panties right on top.

His mom picked them up and held them out to him. "Looking for these?"

He didn't even glance Marcia's way as he snatched the pile and hurried back into the bedroom to find Bailey with a towel wrapped around her.

"That was a quick shower."

"No point delaying the inevitable." She took her clothes and made no comment about how nicely they were folded.

Bailey dressed faster than he'd ever seen a woman do, and then she looked at him. "What's our story? Are we going to tell them about the babies?"

As much as he'd wanted to shout the news from the rooftops yesterday, now he wasn't so sure. Not after seeing the venom in Marcia's eyes.

"Maybe one shock at a time. We'll tell them we're together. Give them a couple of weeks to get used to that, and then give them our wonderful news."

Bailey nodded as if she were cool with this plan (or as cool as she could be in this awkward situation), and then he took her hand and together they walked out to face The Moms.

Quinn addressed their mothers as Bailey lowered herself into the armchair opposite the couch. "Can I get you a tea? Coffee?"

"I couldn't eat or drink a thing, not when I've just discovered you are taking advantage of my daughter in her heartbroken state."

"I'm not heartbroken," Bailey said.

At the same time, his mom piped up. "Now hold your horses, Marcia, I won't have you speaking about my son like that."

"Well, if the shoe fits!"

Nora ignored her friend, looked to Quinn and then to

Bailey. "Just tell me one thing—is this why you broke up with Callum?"

As he waited for Bailey's response, he wondered how his mom would react when she found out they'd betrayed his brother. He wasn't proud of his actions—which reminded him far too much of his dad's indiscretions. He might have a reputation for being a bit of a man about town, but this was the first time he'd done what he did with a woman who wasn't a hundred percent available. He'd always wondered if his mom knew about his dad, but he'd never broached the subject, not wanting to be the one to break her heart.

"I would have ended my relationship with Callum whether Quinn was involved or not," Bailey said. "We weren't right for each other. We had different hopes and dreams, and if you must know, there wasn't any spark."

She looked to Quinn and he could almost *see* the electricity zapping between them.

Marcia rubbed her forehead. "I need something for a headache."

"Don't be so dramatic, Mom," Bailey said, turning back to her mother. "I thought you wanted me to put myself out there again, start dating."

"I didn't mean with someone like *Quinn*."

"How dare you!" Nora turned full-on to face her friend on the couch. Although she'd brandished the wooden spoon a few times when they were kids, Quinn had never seen such rage in her face.

"Oh, come *on*. Everyone knows Quinn's reputation. He's left broken hearts all over town and beyond."

He begged to differ—when he hooked up with a woman, he made sure they knew the score beforehand—but he couldn't get a word in edgewise.

"Maybe he just hadn't met the right woman yet!" yelled his mother.

"*Maybes* aren't good enough where my daughter is concerned!" Marcia shouted, her fists bunching as if she were trying not to use them.

He had a terrible vision of their moms rolling around on the floor, tearing at each other's hair, cat-fighting like a couple of schoolgirls, and him having to pull them apart before they killed each other. As they glowered at each other, he glanced down at Bailey and saw the same fear echoed in her eyes.

I think we should tell them, she mouthed.

He nodded. Things couldn't really get any worse than they already were. Maybe the twins could salvage their moms' friendship. Feuding grandmothers was not what he wanted for his kids.

He took hold of Bailey's hand and cleared his throat, but before he could say anything, she blurted, "We're pregnant! Well, I'm pregnant. But the babies are Quinn's."

"You're what?" Marcia gasped, her hand rushing to cover her mouth.

His mom leaned forward. "Did you say...*babies*?"

"Yes," they chorused.

Then before either mom could recover enough to say another word, Quinn said his piece. "I know you might not think very highly of me, Marcia, but I want you to know I'm a hundred and ten percent committed to your daughter and your grandchildren. I hope that you, and the rest of our families, will understand we never meant to cause any hurt or harm to anyone, and that you'll be able to be happy for us going forward. Because if not, I have no qualms about showing you both the door. I won't have any negativity surrounding Bailey and our children."

He heard Bailey sniff beside him and he thought maybe he'd been too harsh, but when he looked down at her, she was smiling up at him. She held out her hand and he took it, united as they waited for a response.

Marcia was first to break the silence. "Are you going to marry her?"

Quinn squeezed Bailey's hand. The thought of marriage still gave him the heebie-jeebies, but he pasted on a smile. "I'd love to."

"But," Bailey added, "it's not the dark ages and so we're just taking things slowly and seeing where they lead."

Before her mother could respond to that, Nora leaped up from the couch and rushed over to them. She stood in front of him, grabbed him by the ears, pulled him toward her and gave him a big kiss. "I'm so happy I could burst! If Callum wasn't engaged and happy himself, I might have to reprimand you. But it looks to me like things turned out how they are meant to in the end."

Hmm… Quinn wasn't sure Callum would see it like that, but hopefully he'd get over it eventually.

His mom turned and spoke to Bailey. "Congratulations, my darling girl." She stooped and placed her hand against Bailey's stomach. "You look after my grandbabies. Lord knows I've been waiting long enough for some more."

Bailey's mother wasn't quite as enthusiastic. She slowly heaved herself up off the couch and went over to her daughter. She hugged her and congratulated her but barely grunted to him. Was she thinking about Bailey's dad and likening Quinn to him as Bailey had first done?

Whatever. He would win her round just as he had done Bailey and prove to her he was nothing like Marcia's first husband. Or his own father.

Chapter Eight

"You bastard!"

Quinn stumbled back as Callum's fist landed smack in the middle of his face. Pain exploded in his head as blood spurted from his nose. Instinctively he reached his hand up to try to ease the ache. Or was it to clear the mess? He wasn't sure. Fact was, despite the news he'd just landed on his brother, he hadn't expected things to get physical.

For one, Callum's anger seemed a little unreasonable considering Bailey was no longer his girlfriend. And it wasn't like he'd been nursing a broken heart since the breakup. Bailey obviously hadn't been the great love of his life.

For two, Callum had never been the fisticuffs type. He believed words were mightier than the sword, whereas Quinn and his other brothers had been in more brawls in their lives than he could count. They'd disagree, they'd shove each other around, then they'd share a bourbon afterward and all would be forgotten. Once, when they were little, Mac had actually broken Blair's arm; by the time the plaster had set they'd been best buddies again. But Callum had always been too sensible, too mature, too responsible to resort to physical altercations.

The expression on his face now told Quinn his brother was almost as surprised as he was at his actions. He opened his mouth as if to apologize but shut it again immediately, folding his arms over his chest instead and lifting his chin as he narrowed his eyes at Quinn. Callum's anger Quinn could handle, but the hurt he could also see almost broke him. They'd always had a tumultuous relationship, but right now Quinn felt guilt and self-disgust like he'd never felt before.

"It was only one time," he found himself saying. "I swear nothing else happened until you broke up."

Callum raised one of his dark, bushy eyebrows. "And then you discovered she was pregnant?"

Quinn swallowed—trying not to wince as he tasted blood—and lowered his head in one heavy nod.

"I thought you, of all people, would be more careful. If you couldn't keep it in your pants, the least you could have done was to use protection. It's one thing disregarding family so much that you could sleep with my girlfriend, but to take advantage of Bailey like that, I just…" Callum shook his head. "You repulse me!"

"Now just hang on a minute." It was one thing taking a punch to the nose—he probably deserved it—but Quinn wasn't gonna let Callum get away scot-free. "If you don't know why Bailey came running to me, then you're a bigger fool than I thought. If you'd paid more attention to her, actually made her feel like she mattered as much as your work did, then she wouldn't have needed my comfort and support in the first place."

"You're blaming *me* for you accidentally getting my ex pregnant?" Callum blinked. "You're incorrigible."

His guilt was rapidly diminishing. "At least *I'm* doing the right thing by her now."

"And I suppose you want me to give you a gold medal for that? You've well and truly got yourself trapped, haven't you?"

Quinn's hands fisted, but before he could say or *do* anything else, Sophie appeared around Callum's office door. "What on earth is going on in here? We can hear you shouting in the tasting room and it's not good for busi—" Her words faltered and her eyes widened as she registered Quinn's face. He could only imagine what a mess he must look. "Oh, my *God*. Callum, did you *hit* Quinn?"

Callum shrugged one shoulder. "He deserved it."

Her usually smooth brow creasing, Sophie asked, "What did you do?"

"Bailey and I—" Quinn paused to wipe a bit of blood as it trickled down his chin "—we're a couple, and we're having twins."

"Holy macaroni," Sophie said after a few moments' silence. Then she turned and grabbed a box of tissues off Callum's desk. She yanked out a big wad and thrust it at Quinn. "Does Mom know?"

"Thanks." He lifted the tissues and pressed it against his nose. "Yes, we… She and Marcia found out this morning."

"You're just lucky Dad isn't still alive," Callum said. "Mom might think her baby boy can do no wrong, but he'd—"

"Don't bring Dad into this," Quinn warned.

"Don't tell me what to do."

"Now, now, boys." Sophie held a warning hand out to each of them. "This news is…" When she couldn't seem to define it, she changed tack. "Now isn't the time or place to discuss this. We have customers to serve and Quinn's nose needs ice. Callum, I'm guessing you'd rather see to the customers than Quinn?"

Callum made some kind of sound like a wild beast ready to launch at his prey. "I can see to myself," Quinn objected.

Sophie wasn't having any of that. She ordered Callum to summon some professionalism and go out and schmooze with their customers, and then she sneaked Quinn out the back door.

"For a little sister, you're very bossy," he said.

She marched him round the side of the building, ignoring his observation. "So you're the real reason Callum and Bailey split up?"

"No, the writing was on the wall anyway," Quinn said as they turned the corner and walked straight into Mac and Lachlan, who were outside the soon-to-be extended café in deep discussion about the renovations. They stopped talking when they saw Quinn's face.

"Did you walk into a door?" Lachlan grimaced. He'd never been able to stomach blood.

"More likely an irate boyfriend," Mac said, the beginnings of a smirk appearing on his face. He'd barely smiled since coming home last year, so at least one good thing had come from all of this. "Whose toes have you stepped on now?"

"Try an irate brother," Sophie said. "I'm going into the café to grab some ice."

"What did Blair sock you for?" Mac asked, stifling a laugh. "Did you borrow his bagpipes without permission?"

Lachlan snickered like a girl.

"Actually, it was Callum who did the honors." Although Quinn's words were muffled a little by the bloody tissues pressed against his nose, the way they both stopped chuckling made it clear they'd heard. They were likely trying to remember if Mr. Perfect had ever hit anyone else before in his life.

By the time Sophie returned with the ice, Quinn was halfway through telling Mac and Lachlan the whole messy situation.

"I get why he punched you," Lachlan said as Sophie tried to tend to the wound with the ice.

"Ouch," Quinn objected. The ice almost hurt more than the initial blow.

"Really?" Mac mused. "Callum and Bailey were well and truly over before all this came out, so what's the big deal? Aside from the fact that dumb-ass here needs to learn how to change a diaper."

Quinn tried to glare at Mac, but his face had swollen so fast that even doing that hurt. "I know how to change a freaking diaper."

"The big deal is the bro code," Sophie said, and Lachlan nodded. "You don't mess with a friend's or a brother's girl. It would be like me or Annabel stealing each other's boyfriends."

Lachlan nodded, but Mac raised an eyebrow. "You or Annabel would actually have to have a boyfriend for that to be a problem, and I don't recall either of you going on a date since I've been home. I thought you were a lesbian now, anyway."

Sophie poked her tongue out at him. "Like you can

talk. You've barely left your house or have spoken to a woman since you came home."

"I speak to you and Annabel and Mom. Oh, and Chelsea and Bailey."

"We don't count.'

"I guess you're all gonna take his side, then?" Quinn said, Sophie and Mac's bickering amplifying his headache.

Lachlan, Mac and Sophie exchanged glances and then shook their heads.

"Nah," Mac said, speaking for all of them. "Taking sides is too much effort. We'll just bitch about you when we're with Callum and vice versa."

Lachlan lifted his hand and lowered it onto Quinn's shoulder. "We all make stupid mistakes, buddy. The important thing is you're doing the right thing now. And we'll all be there for you and Bailey and our new nieces or nephews."

"Callum will come around eventually," Sophie added. "I'm sure this is something we'll all laugh and joke about at Christmas lunches years from now. And I for one can't wait to be an auntie again."

"Yeah," Mac agreed. "And you guys having twins should keep Mom busy and take the pressure off the rest of us for a while. Well done, little brother." He clapped Quinn on the other shoulder.

"What's going on?" Chelsea appeared behind them. They'd been so consumed by their own conversation they hadn't heard her arrive.

"Oh, my!" She gasped when she looked at Quinn. "What happened to you?"

"Your fiancé," Lachlan informed her.

"What?"

"I've got to get back to the tasting room," Sophie said,

linking her arm through Chelsea's. "Come with. I'll fill you in on the way." Before Chelsea could say another word, Sophie was whisking her away. She called back over her shoulder. "Do you want me to tell Annabel your news, Quinn? I think she's less likely than Callum to get physical, but we shouldn't take any risks. Any more knocks and you won't be the prettiest McKinnel anymore."

As his brothers laughed again, Quinn aimed his middle finger at Sophie. "Go ahead, be my guest. Tell Blair, as well. I've had enough of family for one day."

Right now all he wanted to do was head back to his house and take a good look in the mirror to assess the damage before he met Bailey later in the day to go over some party details. She was stressed enough already about what people might think about their situation, and in wanting to protect her from Callum's wrath, he'd insisted that telling his brother was something he needed to do alone. Now, with his nose throbbing and blood soaking into his favorite T-shirt, he was questioning this decision. If Bailey had been with him, maybe Callum would have showed a little restraint.

"Where are the others?" Bailey asked her mother when they met outside the coffeehouse on the main street of Jewell Rock where she'd been expecting to meet her *whole* family for brunch. This did *not* bode well.

When her mom left Quinn's house a few hours ago, Bailey had suggested they all get together for brunch so she could tell her stepdad and her siblings the good news. In public, and with her younger children in tow, Marcia would be less likely to harp on what she saw as the negatives in this situation. Bailey had hoped that maybe her mother would have mellowed over the last couple of hours, gotten used to the idea of her and Quinn together and maybe even begun to feel excited about becoming a grandmother.

Judging by the still-stern expression on her face, this was a pipe dream.

"I told them when I went home," she said, leaning forward and kissing Bailey on the cheek. There was little warmth in the kiss. "I thought it would be good if we had some mother-daughter alone time to discuss everything."

Oh, boy. With a heavy heart Bailey followed Marcia inside. They sat at a table in the corner and both ordered poached eggs on grilled polenta cakes, even though Bailey was no longer feeling hungry at all. The moment their waitress went off to fill the order, Marcia looked to Bailey across the table and let out a long, heavy sigh.

"Are you sure you're doing the right thing?" She pursed her lips into a fine line as she waited for Bailey to respond.

"Most definitely." There was no point pretending her mom was referring to anything other than the situation with Quinn and the babies. "It was never an option to end the pregnancy or give the babies away."

Marcia looked appalled. "Of course not. I would never suggest that, but Quinn…"

"*Quinn* is my babies' father. He wants to be involved and I'm not going to make that difficult for him."

"Clearly not," Marcia said, a sarcastic edge to her tone. "But I can't help thinking this is history repeating itself. Your father wanted to be involved initially as well, but men are never really ready for fatherhood, even when it's planned. I'm not suggesting you cut Quinn out of your babies' lives, but I have to admit, I'm worried about you giving him any more of yourself. He reminds me too much of your father—he's too good-looking for his own good, as charming as they come, but..."

Bailey didn't want to hear what her mother thought of Quinn, because he *wasn't* like her father and their situations were *not* the same. She held up her hand and cut in before Marcia could say another word. "The pregnancy might have been unplanned, but Quinn wanted to be with me before he found out about the babies. From what you told me about you and my biological father, he took advantage of your teenage crush and then freaked out at the consequences. I know you only want the best for me, Mom, and that you're saying all this with the best intentions, but I'm not nineteen like you were and Quinn isn't a child, either."

"I hope you're right, but I want you to know that if things don't work out with Quinn, then Reginald and I will be here for you and the babies." Her mom reached across the table and squeezed Bailey's hand—for the first time she sounded warm, loving, softer. "I can't wait to be a grandma and Elle is very excited about being an auntie. Dane said you better be having boys."

Bailey summoned a smile and resisted the urge to tug her hand away. "I wish you'd brought them," she said, directing the conversation away from Quinn. "I feel like I haven't seen them for ages."

"Well, you've been busy."

"Yes, I have." She ignored her mother's obvious meaning and instead launched into a spiel about what she'd been up to at the hotel lately.

Their meals arrived and Bailey forced herself to eat as fast as she could so she could make her excuses. She didn't want to linger a moment longer in her mom's pessimistic company.

Why couldn't her mom, of all people, just be happy for her?

Outside on the footpath, she texted Quinn as she walked briskly toward her parked car. She wanted to go back to yesterday, to the excitement of first seeing her babies on the screen and then to the hours following, where she and Quinn had whiled away the time making love and plans for the future.

Have you told everyone? How'd it go?

She beeped her car unlocked, climbed inside and was just turning the key in the ignition when he replied.

Um...

Bailey closed her eyes, sighed, then opened them again and typed another message.

That sounds ominous. Are you home now? I'm coming over.

Sure. I'll see you soon. But don't freak out. I'm okay.

Perplexed at what he could be talking about, she drove as fast as was legal to Quinn's place. He was waiting for her out front. One look at his face and she freaked.

"Oh, my gosh!" she shrieked, reaching out to cup his cheek. He winced as if his whole face, not just his previously beautiful nose, now smashed up and triple the size it used to be, hurt. "Who did this to you?"

He raised an eyebrow, slowly as if even that slight movement caused pain. "Let's see, which one of my brothers might be particularly angry that I'm hooking up with his ex."

She gasped. Of course it had to be Callum, but at the same time, she couldn't imagine him getting this worked up about her. "I'll kill him," she said, surprised by her own rage. "He could barely find the time to spend with me when we were together and now this! Who does he think he is? Why can't our families just get over themselves and play nice?"

"Relax," Quinn said, reaching out to her. He placed his hand on the back of her neck and rubbed gently but firmly, the simple action causing a heady sensation that almost made her forget why she was in a snit. "I'm guessing things didn't go so well with your family this morning?"

She seethed at the memory. "I don't want to talk about it." But then her mouth went directly against the wishes of her brain and spilled out the whole sorry story.

"She'll come round," he said when she'd finished raging. "If not before the babies are born, she'll take one look at their cherubic little faces and forget how they got their start."

"Hmm." Bailey hoped he was right. "But maybe we should cancel your mom's party? Between my mom and Callum, I'm worried there might be a scene and I don't want to ruin Nora's birthday."

"No way." Quinn shook his head adamantly. "Your mom and Callum will just have to accept the way things are now. And I'd like to think that both of them are mature enough to put any grievances aside. We're doing this. We're doing it together. And it's going to be awesome."

Bailey wasn't a hundred percent sure if he was talking about the party now, or parenthood, but either way, she nodded. Quinn was right—the babies and their relationship were a thing. A thing that their families would just have to get used to.

And if they don't? Would she and Quinn survive that? The question was too terrifying to contemplate.

Chapter Nine

"What are you doing? Put that down."

At the sound of Quinn's voice, Bailey looked up from the box she was carrying across the newly erected marquee to see him coming toward her. She stopped walking as he came to a stand in front of her.

"I'm fine. It's not heavy."

"You're carrying my twins," he said, taking the box from her grasp, his hands brushing against hers as they did so. "Any kind of lifting is off limits, especially when I'm around to do it for you."

She rolled her eyes but was secretly pleased by the way he was looking after her. And at least when she didn't have her hands full, she could admire how edible he looked in faded jeans and a long-sleeved T-shirt, pushed up his arms after a couple of hours of exertion. Now that the swelling and bruising had finally gone down on his nose, if anything, he was even better looking than before.

Bailey's mouth watered as an almost irresistible urge to kiss him swept over her. If they weren't in the middle of a marquee, his brothers carrying and positioning the tables and chairs all around them, she would have. Yet, although both their families now knew about their relationship and the babies, and were accepting in various degrees, they'd been "out" for only a few weeks and she wasn't quite ready for public displays of affection, however much her hormones berated her for this reticence.

"Where do you want this?" he asked, a knowing smile on his face as if he could read her illicit thoughts. For a second she had no idea what he was referring to. "The box," he clarified, his tone amused.

"Oh, right. Well, it's got the place cards, the menus and the little goodie bags to go on the tables, so you can put it over by the boxes of tablecloths and cutlery."

"As you wish." Quinn nodded as he headed off in that direction.

Bailey smiled at his *Princess Bride* reference—she'd told him it was her favorite movie, then they'd watched it together, and ever since he'd been quoting Westley every chance he got. It never failed to amuse her. She paused a moment, trying to recall what she'd been up to before he distracted her with his sexiness.

The marquee hire company had arrived mere minutes after Annabel and Sophie had whisked Nora off into town with promises of a long lunch and shopping. As far as they could tell, Nora didn't have a clue about the surprise party. Bailey couldn't wait to see the surprise on her face when she returned later and was greeted by forty of her closest friends and family.

The marquee had been erected without a hitch, and Quinn, Mac and Blair had been carrying tables and chairs over from the café ever since. With Lachlan busy preparing the food, the others were watching Hamish, and even he'd been doing his best to lend a hand, following Quinn and his other uncles around like a shadow. Callum was noticeably absent, having chosen to assist Chelsea and Claire, Blair's ex-wife, who were due to arrive soon with all the decorations. Claire, a florist, was bringing blooms that would brighten up the venue as well as other 1950s paraphernalia to hang on the walls and ceiling.

Bailey had every confidence it was going to look magical, but her stomach did a little tumble at the thought of working alongside Callum and Chelsea. Although they were all making an effort to achieve a new normal that had mostly included avoiding each other, tonight they all had to be in the same space. She prayed Callum and Quinn would think of their mother and refrain from making a scene. One day, she hoped, they'd all be able to be together without any resentment and awkwardness over the fact she'd started out with the wrong brother and that it would be something they could all laugh about. Or, better still, forget.

Aside from this little bit of anxiety, she was feeling on top of the world. True to the books that Quinn had bought, the beginning of the second trimester had signaled the end of her twenty-four-hour morning sickness and a definite increase in her appetite. Not just for food but also for sex, something Quinn had been more than happy to accommodate. Her insides heated at this thought and she felt her cheeks glow as the man in question returned, this time piggybacking Hamish, with Blair and Mac close behind.

"What's next?" Quinn asked as Mac wiped perspiration from his brow.

"Why don't you all go take a break and get a drink?" she suggested. "Then I'll need the stage set up for the band, and the others should be here soon with the flowers and rest of the decorations. How about we reconvene in twenty minutes?"

Mac and Blair didn't need to be asked twice. As they turned and headed toward the exit, Quinn repositioned Hamish on his back and spoke to Bailey. "You should come and put your feet up for a few moments, as well. Let's go see how Lachlan is going in the café. Hamish, how do you feel about a milk shake?"

Quinn's nephew shrieked his affirmative reply and Bailey laughed. Until recently, she hadn't noticed the special bond between these two, but it was just another indication of what kind of dad Quinn would be. She couldn't believe she'd ever doubted him.

She walked beside him and Hamish as they headed the few hundred feet to the café, which was closed today for the party. Mac, in charge of the renovations and extension, had told his mom he needed to do some work that required the closure for the weekend.

As Quinn held open the door for her, Bailey could see that this was a believable excuse. "Wow," she said as she gazed around. The transformation from comfortable café to flash restaurant was well and truly underway. "Mac has been busy, hasn't he?"

"I think work keeps his mind off other things," Quinn said.

He didn't need to state what those other things were. Until last year, Mac had been a professional soccer player, but he'd returned home to lick his wounds after messing up a goal in a big match and the breakup of his long-term relationship that had followed. She wasn't sure if the two things were related, but either way, she felt for him.

Lachlan came out of the kitchen to greet them. Despite this being a family function, he still looked the part in his chef's whites and the hat he'd once told her was called a toque.

"Well, what do you know. It's my favorite son, my favorite brother and…" He stalled a moment and looked to Bailey. "*And* my favorite incubator of my first nieces or nephews."

Bailey shook her head but couldn't help smiling. "You McKinnels are all smooth talkers, aren't you?"

Lachlan grinned back as Hamish rushed over to give him a hug.

"I'm your *only* son," he exclaimed. "And what's an intu-bator?"

"It's something, or some*one* in Bailey's case, that keeps babies safe while they're growing and readying themselves to face the world."

"Bailey's having twins," Hamish said. "Like Hallie and I are twins."

"She sure is."

Quinn took her hand and led her across to a bar stool, one of the only seats still available in the café. The rest of the furniture was now in the marquee. "I'm gonna make milk shakes," he told Lachlan. "That okay with you?"

"Yes, sure, I'm all on track." Lachlan glanced at his watch. "Charlii and Reagan should be here soon."

Charlii and Reagan, who worked in the café, had agreed to do an extra shift for Nora's birthday. Everyone loved the McKinnel matriarch and was only too eager to do anything for her. They'd help Lachlan in the kitchen and then serve the food to the guests in the marquee. A friend of Sophie's and another young girl who worked in the tasting room of the distillery were also coming to serve drinks. Bailey just hoped she hadn't forgotten anything—this was the first event she'd handled entirely on her own, and although it wasn't a huge gig, if the party guests had a good time, then word would spread fast in Jewell Rock.

"I feel a little bad," she said to Lachlan, "that you'll be stuck in here most of the night working and won't be able to properly enjoy your mom's party."

He waved his hand dismissively. "I'll pop my head in when I can, but as long as everyone loves the food, I'll be as happy as Larry."

"If the aromas already wafting out here from the kitchen are anything to go by, I'd say that's a done deal." Even though they'd chosen to continue the 1950s theme with the food—alcoholic milk shakes and root beer floats, cheeseburgers, hot dogs and fries on the menu—with Lachlan catering they wouldn't just be your run-of-the-mill diner cuisine.

He beamed at the compliment and then lifted Hamish onto the stool beside Bailey. "You felt them move yet?" he asked, nodding toward her stomach.

"I'm not sure. The books say it's still too early, but I swear I've felt the odd flutter."

"Danielle felt movement early with the twins, as well," he said. "I guess when there are two babies in there, it's a bit more cramped, so everything is amplified."

Bailey nodded, wanting to ask Lachlan other things about his ex-wife's pregnancy but biting her tongue for fear of upsetting him in front of Hamish. She'd never known Danielle well, having still been in high school herself when the marriage had gone sour, but everyone knew his wife had left because she couldn't handle mothering a special-needs child, so she'd left Hamish with Lachlan and taken their daughter. Already blissfully, head over heels in love with the two little strangers inside her, Bailey couldn't comprehend how any mother could ever find her child lacking. But Danielle was the one missing out—Hamish was a great kid and he'd make a great cousin to her babies.

"When are you finishing up at the restaurant?" she asked Lachlan, even though she already knew the answer from talking about the distillery to Quinn.

"At the end of the month. Mac should have the construction finished, so there'll be plenty to keep me busy getting ready for our grand opening here in June."

"I can already tell it's going to be wonderful."

They talked a little more about the plans for the distillery's new restaurant, while Hamish drew chess pieces on a napkin beside them. When Quinn returned with the milk shakes, the conversation returned to the party until it was time to head back to the marquee.

Quinn hitched Hamish onto his back again and they farewelled Lachlan, making him promise to come and ask for help if he needed it. As they walked toward the marquee, Bailey saw that Claire, Callum and Chelsea had arrived. Quinn's brothers were helping unload Claire's florist van.

"Hi, guys," Bailey said as they approached the activity. "Wow, those flowers look gorgeous."

"Only the best for my ex-mother-in-law." Claire, who'd been like a sister to her the last five years, grinned as she thrust a bucket full of magnolias into Blair's arms. "Wow. Look at you, Bailey, you're already showing."

She flushed and instinctively placed a hand against her

stomach. "I know," she said, careful not to look at Callum. "I feel massive already, and I'm not even halfway to term."

Chelsea offered her a genuine smile. "Pregnancy suits you. You look gorgeous."

At the other woman's warm words, tears welled up in Bailey's eyes and she smiled back. Maybe if she and Chelsea could get past the weirdness of their situation, Callum and Quinn would follow suit. "Thank you," she managed.

After that, there was no more time for contemplation. Together Bailey, Chelsea and Claire arranged the flowers and decorated the tables to a standard all three perfectionists were happy with. In keeping with the theme, they had black-and-white checkered tablecloths, place mats that looked like old vinyl records, cotton-pink chair covers and a black poodle centerpiece on every table. The little guest gifts were small boxes of popcorn.

Meanwhile the guys worked tirelessly hanging disco balls across the marquee and black music notes on the walls, and building a temporary stage for the band. When they'd finished, Bailey couldn't have been more pleased. Alongside the makeshift dance floor was the jukebox they'd hired—loaded with the best of Buddy Holly, Chuck Berry, Johnny Cash, Elvis Presley and the like—for those who wanted to continue reveling after the band stopped. Bailey reckoned she'd be lucky to make it to ten o'clock, but knowing that once the babies arrived her social life would become nonexistent, she planned on giving it her best shot.

"Surprise!" shouted the forty-odd guests as Sophie and Annabel led a blindfolded Nora into the marquee just after seven o'clock that night.

The band, who'd gone quiet when Bailey received the

text message from Sophie that arrival was imminent, launched up again, channeling Jerry Lee Lewis as Nora's eyes boggled and her mouth fell open.

"Happy Birthday!" shouted all the guests.

"Oh, my Lord," Nora exclaimed, her hand pressed against her chest. Tears sprouted from her eyes, but the grin on her face told Bailey they were happy ones.

She glanced at Quinn standing beside her and smiled victoriously. "We did it."

"We sure did," he said, pulling her into his side, "and now it's time to enjoy the party."

"Not so fast." She laughed, pulling away from him. "We need to get your mom and sisters into costume and, as this is my event, I can't relax—I have to oversee it all."

Before Quinn could object she went over to greet Nora. "Happy Birthday," she said, leaning forward to hug her.

"She had no idea," Sophie said, smiling at Bailey.

"She wondered why the two of us—who usually aren't that fussed about shopping—kept wanting to go into *just one more shop*," added Annabel.

"I should have known something was up." Nora glanced around, taking in her friends—all grinning and waving at her—and the theme-decorated marquee. Then she looked back to Bailey. "Were you responsible for all of this?"

"It was Quinn's idea," Bailey said. "He wanted to make it special for you, and we had a lot of help from everyone else. In the end it was a team effort."

"It's lucky I didn't have a heart attack. But look at you all, dressed up in costume—I wish I'd known. I love fancy dress."

"And Bailey has that covered as well, Mom," said Annabel, who was for once wearing a skirt and top. As a local firefighter, she was a bit of a tomboy and was rarely seen in anything but jeans and T-shirt, but she scrubbed up nicely.

Bailey and the twins whisked Nora over to the corner of the marquee where the photo booth they'd organized was waiting for Nora to use as a changing room. They'd gathered a number of different outfits for her to choose from.

"Oh, my," she exclaimed as they showed her through her choices. "Is there anything you haven't thought of?"

Bailey smiled at the compliment. Nora chose a very elegant swing dress, black at the top with a bright red full skirt. The black heels she'd been wearing that day matched perfectly and her daughters insisted on her wearing a ginger wig that was styled in the classic 1950s bubble cut. For an outfit thrown together in a few moments, she looked amazing.

The evening progressed and everyone seemed to be enjoying themselves, devouring Lachlan's gourmet burgers and bopping along to the band. Bailey's feet ached from being on them almost nonstop all day, but inside she buzzed from the thrill of organizing a successful event. Normally, when planning events at work for the hotel, she had to run everything by her boss first, but she'd loved being the one calling the shots this time, and it only made her more determined to start her own event-planning business.

She'd take maternity leave from the hotel and use the time—if there was any when you had newborn twins—to write a business plan and work out her game plan.

Her thoughts were interrupted as she felt someone come up beside her. She turned to see her mother and tried not to let her disappointment show.

"Hi, Mom. Hope you're enjoying yourself. Reginald seems to be having fun." *And I hope you're planning on keeping your negative thoughts to yourself.* She nodded toward the dance floor, where her stepfather looked to be taking lessons from his eleven-year-old son. Beside them, Quinn twirled Bailey's thirteen-year-old half sister, Elle, under his arm.

But her Mom surprised her. "I truly am enjoying myself. And Nora hasn't smiled so much in months. You and Quinn have certainly done a good job. You obviously make a good team. I'm sorry if I've been less than enthusiastic up until now, but it's only because I love you and I want the best for you."

"I know, Mom, thank you." Bailey gave her a hug, and when they pulled back, Quinn was striding toward them. Poor guy knew her mother didn't think the highest of him and she guessed he'd seen them talking and come to rescue her.

"Hey," she said as he approached.

"Hey, yourself." He kissed her on the cheek, pulled her into his side and flashed her mother a smile. "Hi, Marcia, I hope you're enjoying the party."

"I am." She returned a genuine smile. "I was just telling Bailey what a wonderful job the two of you have done together."

"Really?" Quinn raised an eyebrow, his skepticism evident in his tone. "That's great. I hope you won't mind if I whisk this one away for a dance before your other daughter completely tires me out."

Marcia laughed and shooed them with her hands. "Go. Have fun."

Her hand in his, Bailey followed Quinn onto the dance floor and relaxed into his arms. Although the song had an upbeat tempo, Quinn held her close and they swayed gently together. She'd never imagined it was possible to feel this happy, but right now her heart felt so full that her lungs were struggling to find the room to breathe. It wasn't only the babies she'd fallen in love with—Quinn had snuck under her skin, crawled into her heart and set up residence there, as well.

"Is your mom drunk?" he whispered, his lips right against her ear.

She laughed and was about to tell him about their conversation, but a shriek escaped her mouth instead as she felt a definite movement inside her.

"Are you okay?" Quinn pulled back, concern etched into his gorgeous face as he looked down into hers.

"Yes." She nodded, blinking as her hand rushed to her stomach. "I've been feeling these flutters the last few days. I thought it was too early and I must be imagining things, but I just felt something really strong."

"Seriously?" He pressed his hand against her belly.

They both froze a few moments, waiting and hoping for more movement that Quinn could also feel, but if she *had* felt the babies, they'd now gone back to sleep. "I'm sorry." She sighed, disappointed he hadn't been able to share in the joyful moment.

"Don't be. There'll be plenty more opportunities." His brow creased a little. "You're looking really tired."

"Jeez, thanks. You know how to make a lady feel special."

He ignored her attempt at humor, took her hand and led her off the dance floor. "You've been so busy today, maybe you should take a load off and put your feet up."

She was about to argue that she felt perfectly fine, but a yawn escaped her mouth that would prove her a liar. "I suppose a few moments sitting down wouldn't do any harm."

Quinn deposited her at their table. "I'll go get you a drink," he said, before turning and heading over to the bar.

His leather jacket was on the back of the seat beside her and she couldn't resist grabbing it and putting it on. It wasn't that she was cold—impossible after being pressed up against his warm body on the dance floor—but that having it next to her skin was the next best thing to having him. A contented smile on her face, she sat back in the chair. It had been the perfect night, she thought as she slipped her hands into his pockets. One was empty, but the other had a crumpled piece of paper inside.

Without thinking, she pulled it out and unfolded it.

"No!" Her whole body went cold as she stared down at a letter she'd never expected to see again. The letter she'd anonymously sent to Aunt Bossy. Her words now wobbled in her hand like a nightmare come back to haunt her. No wonder an answer had never been published in the paper. But how on earth had Quinn got hold of it? While she couldn't make sense of that, a heavy realization landed in her heart. Somehow her letter *had* found its way into his possession and *he knew*.

He'd always known.

She'd never imagined the possibility of Quinn reading the column, never mind the actual letter. But as she read over it now, she saw that reading this he would have immediately guessed the situation to be theirs. The timing and the bit about her ex, her description of her baby's father and not knowing whether he was reliable...

For a second, she felt sadness and guilt at the thought of him knowing her low opinion of him, but then she realized that he'd tricked her. She had no idea how the letter had come into his possession, but the way the paper was crumpled indicated it had been read over and over again, folded and refolded, and then stashed in his pocket for ages.

Nausea that this time she couldn't blame on the babies swirled in her stomach as she remembered the Friday night Quinn had turned up on her doorstep out of the blue. Exactly a day after she'd sent her Aunt Bossy letter. She *had* been skeptical; his sudden interest seemed too good to be true. But stupidly wanting to believe he had feelings for her, she'd clutched at straws and ignored the blatant signs that something was up.

Oh, God, what a fool. Quinn would never have begun something serious with her if she hadn't gotten pregnant. He was obviously only with her out of some kind of sense of duty. She hadn't been able to truly win Callum's heart, so how could she think there was anything that special about her that would turn his Casanova younger brother from his serial-dating ways?

With that thought, tears sprouted in her eyes. She shoved back her seat, scrambled to stand and almost tripped over her own feet in her efforts to escape the marquee.

Damn Quinn and damn his family. She wished their moms had never met!

Chapter Ten

As Quinn wove through the tables on his way back from the bar, a number of family friends stopped to congratulate him on his impending fatherhood. He smiled politely as he listened to snatches of parenting advice, when all he wanted was to get back to check on Bailey. She'd done an awesome job organizing tonight, but she'd barely taken a breather all day, and when they'd been dancing, she'd looked as if she might fall asleep on her feet at any moment.

Finally, he made it past the dance floor, then kept his head down so as not to make eye contact with anyone else as he headed for their table. A few feet away, he looked up only to find an empty seat where he'd left her sitting. He cursed and glanced around, guessing she must have found some little party detail to attend to. When he couldn't immediately locate her, he put her ice-cream soda down on the table so he could go look for her.

And that was when his gaze caught on the letter on the table.

Another curse word—harsher than the first—escaped his lips as he noticed his leather jacket missing from the back of his seat. He hadn't worn the jacket for a while, but he'd put it on tonight as part of his costume, having totally forgotten stashing the letter in his pocket that day Bailey had come into his office.

He knew immediately how this was going to look.

Sweat beading on his forehead and his heart thumping, he strode back through the party-goers, this time ignoring all attempts to solicit his attention.

"Have you seen Bailey?" he asked his sisters as they moved their bodies on the dance floor to the sounds of Elvis.

Sophie shook her head, but Annabel pointed to the entrance of the marquee. "I think I saw her leave a few minutes ago. She's probably gone to use the restroom."

Quinn hurried outside into the night and scanned left and right. To one side of the tent the distillery grounds were pitch-black except for a few stars glittering in the sky above. On the other side lights shone from the tasting room, which was open so the party guests could use the restrooms. Leaving the noise and music of the party behind him, he ran toward the building.

Inside, he found the place deserted. Lachlan had long ago finished his chef duties and was now in the tent partying with everyone else. Quinn rapped on the door of the women's bathroom, and when there was no reply, he marched straight on in. The three cubicles were all empty and he felt like kicking something as he turned to leave. He tried the men's, just in case, but that, too, was empty.

Where the hell is she?

As he stepped back out into the night, he thought of his phone. If she'd put two and two together about the letter, she might not answer him, but… Before he could even finish the thought, he'd whipped his cell out of his pocket and pressed Bailey on speed dial. He stilled and listened, his heartbeat thrumming loudly in his ears as he waited. Then, *bingo*. In the distance, toward the chief distillery building, he heard the faint ringing of a phone.

Less than thirty seconds later, he found her, crumpled on the ground, leaning back against a big wooden pillar. The only light came from the screens of their cell phones and the moon, but his eyes acclimatized quickly. She was wearing his leather jacket and her mascara had drawn black lines down her face. The word *broken* came to mind and he hoped more than anything he had the power to fix this.

He dropped down to his knees in front of her and instinctively reached out, wanting to hold her, but she pushed him away, like she couldn't bear his touch.

"How…? Where…where did you get that letter?"

Quinn took a quick breath. "Surprise! You're looking at Aunt Bossy." It was the first time he'd ever told anyone about his secret alter ego, and he tried to make light of it, but not even a shadow of a smile crossed Bailey's face.

Instead, her mouth dropped open and she looked at him as if he were a stranger.

"You remember Trevor from school?" he asked, trying to fill the silence, hoping he'd be able to distract her from her obvious anger. She didn't nod, but he could tell by the expression in her eyes that she did, and he continued anyway. He told her about how when Trevor had first started at the local paper, he'd wanted to shake things up a bit, to make his mark, and Quinn had joked that he needed one of those columns—like the famous Dear Abby and Ann Landers. There was nothing people liked better than reading about other people's dramas—it made them feel better about their own lives.

"Anyway, Trevor loved the idea, but he had no idea about how to find someone to fill the position. I told him to do it himself, but he dared me to give it a shot. As a nineteen-year-old boy, I thought I had all the answers to all the problems of the world, so I accepted the challenge. In the early days, I channeled Mom and tried to work out what she'd say in response to the letters I received. After a while, I found giving other people advice about their lives came easy to me. And the more I did it, the more rewarding it became."

Quinn wasn't sure if Bailey had registered a word he'd said. He wished she'd say something, but when she didn't, he continued. "You wouldn't believe the number of follow-up letters I've had, people telling me how much my advice helped. I've never had a problem answering a letter until yours turned up. I've got to admit, that one threw me. I guessed almost immediately it was about us and—"

"And you decided to deceive me!" Bailey narrowed her eyes at him. "The right thing to do when you got that letter would have been to come talk to me about it. Instead, you lied. You made up some ridiculous party excuse to spend time with me and then pretended you actually cared, that you actually wanted us to be together."

He tried to keep his voice calm as he replied. "What options did you give me, Bailey? In your letter you made it clear you didn't think me up to the task of parenting. You weren't even sure you wanted to tell me. If I confronted you, you'd have just pushed me away. I couldn't risk that. Instead, I chose to prove to you that I wasn't who you thought I was. That I—"

"Yet you're exactly who I thought you were," she interrupted. "A liar, someone who plays games and can't take anything or *anyone* seriously."

"That's not true," he said, trying again to reach out to her. "This wasn't a game. You're not a game to me." This was the most serious thing he'd done in his life.

She flapped her hands at him, as if he were a bothersome insect. "I knew this was too good to be true. If it weren't for the babies, you'd never have come to me. My mom was right. Everyone was right about you, about us. You've made me a fool. I'm going to be the laughingstock of Jewell Rock. The stupid woman who thought Quinn might actually like her. Maybe even *love* her."

Discomfort at the word *love* washed over him, but he refused to let it show. "It doesn't have to be like that," he said. "We don't have to tell anyone anything. You and I have chemistry in spades, we're friends and we're having twins together—what better foundation is there for marriage? We both made errors of judgment, but at least everything's out in the open now. We can start afresh properly. Marry me!"

Bailey was silent a few moments, her mouth gaping open so wide he could see her tonsils in the moonlight. "Are you insane?" she shouted. "I've just narrowly escaped one loveless marriage, I'd be a bigger fool than I already am to walk straight into another."

The temper he'd been barely restraining since she'd accused him of being a liar broke loose. "You're too idealistic and romantic for your own good. Maybe you should watch less *Princess Bride* and more daytime talk shows. Real life isn't a fairy tale."

A tear trickled down her cheek as she shook her head slowly at him. "How can you be such a cynic when you were brought up in such a warm, loving family?"

"Warm, loving family? What a joke! My family is exactly why I'm the way I am. You know that marriage between my parents you think is the bee's knees? It was a farce. My father was a cheating scumbag who knew nothing about love."

She gasped. And at the same moment he inwardly cursed himself for letting loose this nugget of information.

"Look, I understand you're upset," he said, wanting to distract her from what he'd just said. He dug his handkerchief out of his pocket—something he rarely used but carried out of habit thanks to his mom, who'd insisted it was something all men should have. "But we should be getting back to the party before somebody notices we're missing."

"I'm not going back!" Despite the tears now pouring down her cheeks, Bailey rejected his offer of the handkerchief and heaved herself up off the ground. He followed suit, snapping to his feet as she shouted at him. "I don't want to see anyone. I don't want to talk to anyone! This party was your idea—you go and finish it off. If anyone asks where I am, tell them I was tired and went home to bed."

With that, she shoved past him and started running toward the parking lot. He didn't hurry after her as he instinctively wanted to do because he feared that might only make her run faster and he didn't want to increase her chances of falling. Just the thought of her tripping and causing harm to the babies made Quinn's pulse race so fast he could hear it thrashing in his ears. He stood there, frozen in front of the distillery, wondering how his life had gone to hell in a handbasket so damn quickly.

If only he'd burned that stupid letter. If only he hadn't taken off his jacket. If only he'd come clean in the beginning.

If only...he hadn't slept with Bailey in the first place.

Cursing every foolish decision he'd made in the last few months, he kicked his foot against the side of the wooden pillar. The last thing he wanted to do right now was head back to the party and pretend everything was okay, but he didn't see he had any option. He didn't want to spoil his mom's night and he had to make excuses for Bailey before suspicions were raised.

With a heavy heart and a tight gut, he strode back across the grass. Inside, the party still raged, everyone dancing and smiling as if the world was exactly how it should be, but his world had never felt more off-kilter. He wound through the revelers straight over to the bar and demanded a double shot of whiskey. He'd barely lifted the glass to his lips when a hand came crashing down on his shoulder and he jolted, splashing alcohol all over his fingers.

He turned his head ready to rage at whoever had made him spill his drink, only to find Callum standing beside him, smiling at him in a way he hadn't for a long while. Still able to feel the pain in his nose from its introduction to Callum's fist a few weeks ago, Quinn found himself suspicious. Did Callum know what had just happened between him and Bailey? Was he here to gloat?

"What do you want?" Quinn grunted. "I really don't need your crap right now. It's Mom's birthday and if you—"

"Little brother, *chill*," Callum said, still grinning.

Quinn couldn't recall a time his older brother had ever used the word *chill* in that context before. "I'm here to offer an olive branch." He turned to the chick behind the bar. "Can I have one of those as well, please?"

"How much have you had to drink?" Quinn asked and then took a sip of his own.

Callum chuckled, nodded his thanks to the barwoman as she handed him a glass and then looked back to Quinn. "I wanted to say I'm happy for you."

Quinn blinked in surprise.

"Watching you and Bailey together today and tonight, I can tell what you've got going between you is the real deal," he said. "I can see you really love her and that I overreacted when I found out about the two of you."

Love? Quinn didn't know what to say to that, so he took another sip of his drink.

"I never really understood what the big deal was about love until I met Chelsea," Callum said, "and then in a matter of days she turned my world upside down. That happened at a time when I didn't even think I wanted or had time for a relationship, but you don't choose love, it chooses you. It just happens and you can't control it, even if you try."

Quinn raised an eyebrow, thinking his brother must have been watching the same movies as Bailey. "That's really deep, man."

Callum elbowed him in the side. "Will you stop mocking me while I'm trying to have a serious conversation?"

"Right. Sorry." Quinn happily let his forced smile fall from his face.

"I know you and Bailey don't need my blessing, but I wanted you to know you've got it anyway. I'm so happy with Chelsea, how could I begrudge the same happiness for my old friend and my little brother? Besides, I want my kid to grow up with his cousins, since they'll only be a couple of months apart in age."

It took a few moments for Quinn to catch on. *Were Callum and Chelsea...?* He shook his head slightly, distracted momentarily from his current sticky predicament. "Are you guys having a baby?"

"Shh. Keep your voice down. It's very early days. Chelsea only just found out this week and she doesn't want to say anything yet, but I've been bursting to tell someone. I figured you might understand."

"Jeez." No wonder Callum had mellowed. "Wow. Yeah. I do." Quinn thought of the ultrasound images now permanently imprinted on his brain. "There's nothing like it, is there? Congratulations." He tried to sound happy for his brother, when inside something squeezed at the fact that once again Callum had the whole damn package, whereas he'd screwed everything up.

"Thanks." Callum grinned, thankfully oblivious to Quinn's discomfiture. "There must be something in the water around here, hey?"

Quinn nodded and forced a laugh in reply.

"Are you and Bailey going to find out the sex?" Callum asked. "It's something Chelsea and I can't agree on. She wants a surprise, but I kinda like the idea of knowing so we can make better plans."

"Of course you do." Callum had always been Mr. Organized and Controlled; he'd known he was going to be a dad five minutes and already he was thinking ahead. "Actually," Quinn said, "we've talked about it a lot and have decided we'd rather not know. Everything about our relationship has been a surprise so far. Why not this?"

"I see your point, but I don't have the patience for surprises," Callum said as Chelsea came up beside them. He turned to his future wife, the mother of his unborn child, and drew her into his side. Quinn had to admit, they did look perfect together.

Was that what Callum saw when he looked at Quinn and Bailey together? Without a doubt his attraction to Bailey was off the charts. And he enjoyed her company, enjoyed spending time with her more than he did any other person on the planet. She made him laugh, she made him *feel*, she made him want to be a better man.

Did all that equate to love?

Chapter Eleven

Grass and then the gravel crunching under her feet, Bailey didn't stop running until she reached Quinn's SUV parked in the lot. Dragging his keys out of his jacket pocket, she beeped it open, climbed up into the driver's seat, pulled the door shut and locked it behind her, all the while gasping for air as her lungs recovered from her mad dash away from him.

It was bad enough that she'd succumbed to tears in his presence, but she didn't want his pity. Didn't want to hear whatever pathetic excuse he'd try to use to justify what he'd done. If he even cared a little, wouldn't he have chased after her? She glanced out the window, both relieved and utterly gutted to see that he hadn't. With a fleeting thought to her purse and cell phone still in the marquee, she put the key in the ignition and started the vehicle. With the seat far back to accommodate Quinn's height, she could barely reach the pedals, but the moment she adjusted it to suit her, she couldn't get out of the parking lot fast enough.

And the best thing about taking his transport was that he wouldn't easily be able to follow, not that it looked like he planned to.

She swallowed the hurt that caused and then tore over the bridge that crossed the beautiful lake in front of the distillery. Swerving onto the main road, she narrowly missed a raccoon as it skidded in front of her. Damn Quinn—not only was he messing with her life and her heart, now he was almost aiding and abetting the murder of cute, innocent forest animals. She slowed the vehicle and tried to do the same with her breathing, glad there weren't many others on the road as she took the backstreets to her house. But it was hard to calm herself with her head so full of rage and anguish.

Quinn was Aunt Bossy? His dad had cheated on his mom? None of it made any sense whatsoever.

If the latter were true, why had Callum never mentioned it? They may have drifted apart in the last few months, but they'd been close once; he'd confided in her about other stuff. And why hadn't her own mom ever said anything? Had Nora ever even told her friend? On the one hand, Bailey couldn't wrap her head around this news—it simply didn't compute—but on the other hand, it did. Quinn's knowledge that his parents' marriage wasn't what they made it out to be, wasn't the perfection everyone thought it was, could account for why he'd so ardently avoided the institution. Hadn't he all but said that when she'd called him on his cynicism?

But whether it was true or not didn't change the fact that Quinn hadn't come chasing her out of any desperate need inside him. He hadn't pursued her because he couldn't get enough of her, couldn't get her out of his head, because he was falling in love with her. The real Quinn had turned her away when she'd come looking for more the day after Thanksgiving; the real Quinn was with Bailey only out of a sense of duty.

Well, screw the real Quinn. It was the twenty-first century. She had a roof over her head and a good job. She could do motherhood perfectly well on her own.

Yet, no matter the bravado Bailey tried to fool herself with, she couldn't deny the ache that the truth about Quinn had brought upon her. It wasn't just an empty gaping hole in her heart but physical pain all over her body, as if she'd suddenly come down with a killer flu. She wanted to climb into bed, wrap the blankets around her, bury herself there and fall into some kind of oblivious slumber.

With this thought, she parked the SUV in front of her apartment block and dragged herself out and up the path toward the front door. But the relief she expected when she stepped inside and locked the door behind her didn't come. The place no longer felt like home. Perhaps because for the last couple of weeks she'd barely been there—having spent almost every night and weekend at Quinn's place, which was bigger and nicer than her poky apartment. Although they hadn't officially made plans about her moving in, he'd alluded to it many times and they'd been in discussions about turning his spare room—currently cluttered with bike parts and old sporting trophies—into a nursery.

Stupid, stupid, stupid, deceitful discussions.

She swiped at the tears still barreling down her face, angry at herself that she couldn't just switch them off. She didn't want to feel anything for Quinn Jerkface McKinnel. Realizing she was still wearing his jacket and that being able to smell him on it probably wasn't helping, Bailey tore it off and hurled it across the living room. Exhausted, she flopped down onto the couch and sat there, frozen, for a few moments, until her gaze caught on the pile of old newspapers on the coffee table. For a while, she'd bought the *Bulletin* religiously, scouring Aunt Bossy's column for a reply to her letter. Tonight the reason she'd never found one had become perfectly clear.

Knowing it probably wouldn't help her anger or heartbreak, Bailey leaned over and snatched the first newspaper off the top. She quickly found the Aunt Bossy page and, without even reading the letter, snapped straight to Quinn's reply.

Dear Second Fiddle:
Do not be a Princess Diana with three people in your marriage. You need to take charge and do something about this situation before your resentment builds up to a bursting point.

Yes, your husband needs to man up and put you before his mother, but you need to take some responsibility in this situation, as well. Does he see what is happening? Have you spoken to him about the situation? If not, it's time to tell him how you feel—men are not mind readers—tell him that you need him to cut the apron strings from Mommy Dear.

Ultimatums may not be nice, but in this situation, I think it's fair you make one...

As she read the column, Bailey wondered how she had never guessed it was Quinn? It now seemed so blatantly

obvious. She could hear his voice in every word and wondered what all Aunt Bossy's devoted fans would think if
they knew *she* was really a twenty-seven-year-old male
who had no experience whatsoever with any of the issues
he wrote about. He'd have been better suited to write a
column advising other guys on how to pick up chicks!

But even as she thought this, she had to admit Quinn's
advice in the column had always been spot-on. Well
thought out, succinct replies with a dash of humor and
just enough heart to make the reader feel as if the writer
really cared. It was why she'd written her letter in the
first place.

Hah! What a joke!

She needed to rid her personal space of all things
Quinn—the newspapers, his leather jacket, they all had
to go. After heaving herself off the couch, she picked up
his jacket and the pile of papers. The plan had been to
dump everything in the trash—the thought of Quinn's
beloved jacket bespeckled with moldy food marginally
elevated her mood—but outside in the fresh evening air,
something snapped inside of her. She walked straight past
the bin and out onto the communal lawn at the side of the
apartment, where she dumped the newspapers and jacket
in a pile. Then, smiling for the first time since she'd found
the letter, she rushed back inside to fetch some matches.

It would be much more cathartic to watch all things
Quinn going up in smoke. More terminal.

For someone normally tidy and organized, it took Bailey over ten minutes to find the matches. As she stormed
around opening cupboards and drawers, she blamed pregnancy brain, for which she could also lay the blame on
Quinn. The moment she located the matches, she hurried

back outside and, without a moment's hesitation, struck the match against the box and tossed it on top of the pile.

She stood back a little and watched as the flame took hold.

"What on earth are you doing?" came a voice from the open window of one of the apartments above.

Without glancing upward, she waved her hand in dismissal and called out, "I've got it under control. Go back to bed."

And she did. The hose was only a few feet away. It wasn't the middle of summer. The fire at her feet was about the only thing she *did* have control of in her life and she wasn't going to let anyone interrupt it. Waiting for a feeling of satisfaction to overcome her, she watched the flames and listened to the crackling of the burning newspaper and leather—the only sounds in an otherwise peaceful Jewell Rock night.

Until the noise of a motorbike approaching interrupted her quiet reflection.

She tensed and turned toward the road. It couldn't be Quinn because he'd sold his bike almost two months ago. Yet, when the vehicle came to a stop only a few yards away from her, even before its rider tore the helmet from his head, she knew it *was* him. Without his leather jacket, the white shirt he'd been wearing for the party did nothing to hide the muscles she'd become so intimately acquainted with. Despite herself, her mouth watered at the sight, but as he lifted one lean thigh over the bike to get off, she remembered that what he looked like didn't mean a blasted thing. His sex appeal had never been up for debate—*that* had been what got her into trouble in the first place. It was his scruples, his deception, she had issue with.

"When I said I didn't want to talk to anyone, that most definitely included you," she shouted, holding out a hand to warn him off as he approached.

He looked past her to the fire. Before she could reply, he jogged over to the hose, turned it on and aimed it at the flames.

She sighed as she watched him drown the fire. So much for not letting anyone interrupt her efforts. Too bad he wasn't in time to save his jacket.

"What the hell were you doing?" he asked, once there was nothing but a soggy mess left on the grass. "Is that my jacket?"

"Was," she replied with a shrug of her shoulders.

"You could have set fire to the whole building. I thought you didn't want to be the laughingstock of Jewell Rock? If the fire department were called, Annabel would definitely have found out."

"You know what, Quinn? I don't have the energy to care about any of that anymore. I'm over people lying to me and I'm not going to lie to anyone else. Unlike some people I know." She folded her arms over her chest and glared at him. "How can you sleep at night?"

He held up his hands in surrender. "I'm sorry. It was wrong not to tell you I knew about the letter."

It was clear from the tone of his voice he didn't think it as wrong as she did. That he thought his deception perfectly acceptable because she hadn't told *him* the second she'd found out she was pregnant. Well, he couldn't blame hormones for his misjudgment.

"I wasn't simply talking about us," she said. "I'm not the only one you've fooled pretending to be someone you're not. How do you think all your readers would feel if they found out who Aunt Bossy was?"

"Do you really think any advice columnists are exactly who they say they are? I give the best advice I can and as I said, I've had plenty of thank-you letters from happy readers. I think the advice, not the person who gives it, is the most important thing."

She pursed her lips. Perhaps he had a point, but that was *beside* the point. Nodding her head toward the bike parked alongside the curb, she said, "You lied to me about selling your bike, as well. Made me think you were making all these sacrifices for our babies."

"So now you *are* talking about us?" Quinn threw up his hands. "I can't keep up. And I never lied. I said I bought a car. I didn't say I sold the bike. It's been at the distillery all along. Which is a damn good thing considering you stole my car tonight."

Annoyance that he was annoyed with her flared within her. She'd had enough of this conversation. She'd had enough of him. She was desperately trying to hold on to her anger for fear of breaking into tears again in front of him, but if he stayed any longer, she'd turn into a blubbering mess. Again. She'd cried more over Quinn in the last hour than she had over the end of her five-year relationship with Callum.

"Whatever. Can you please go now?"

Quinn hadn't meant to storm over to Bailey's place and go off at her. But he also hadn't been expecting to find her outside setting his favorite jacket alight. Not that he cared about the jacket; it was the possibility of her burning herself that gave him heartburn. Pregnant hormonal women were a danger to themselves and to society. It was impossible to reason with them. But this wasn't just any pregnant hormonal woman, this was Bailey—the mother of his babies, his woman.

When he'd come round the corner, seen the smoke and Bailey standing next to the roaring flames, he'd almost come off his bike in his efforts to get to her. The thought of something bad happening to her was unlike any fear he'd ever felt. And the magnitude of his feelings hit him like a bolt of lightning.

Callum was right—he did love her. There was no other explanation.

His chest squeezed. It felt like the smoke in the air was suffocating him.

It may have been the babies who made him sit up and take notice, but he suddenly knew with absolute certainty that if she lost the twins tomorrow he would still want to be with her over anybody else.

Somehow he had to make Bailey see reason, but he wasn't going to air their dirty laundry out here on the grass for the viewing pleasure of all her neighbors. "How about we go inside and talk?" he said, as calmly as he could.

"Are you deaf?" she asked, not calm at all. "I said I didn't want to talk to you. Now go home and let me go inside and get some sleep."

He highly doubted she'd be able to sleep so worked up—he knew he wouldn't—but he knew better than to say so. Still, he wasn't going to walk away without telling her how he really felt. "Can I have my car keys first?"

She sighed and, without another word, turned and started back toward the building. He took this as an invitation to follow her to her front door, which she'd left wide-open.

"You really should be careful about leaving your apartment unlocked like this," he said, following her inside.

"Don't tell me what I should and shouldn't do." She sniffed and held up her hand. "And stay right there, you're not welcome any further."

As much as he wanted to step right up to her and pull her into his arms and show her rather than tell her how he felt, he stopped just inside the doorway and didn't move so much as a toe. Bailey went into the living room and returned a few moments later with his car keys.

She all but threw them at him, and as he caught them, he started talking. "I know you don't want to hear any of this, but I can't leave until I've said it. So if you want me out of your face, I suggest you listen up."

Bailey's eyes widened, but when she opened her mouth as if to object, he kicked the front door shut behind him. She closed her mouth again, seemingly resigned to his terms, but didn't invite him in any further.

He sucked in a breath and shoved his hands in his pockets so she couldn't see them shaking. "When I was sixteen, Dad was working late one day and Mom asked me to go across to the distillery to tell him dinner was ready. I jumped at the chance, as I loved every minute I spent there, soaking in as much about whiskey and the family business as I could. Even though I wasn't allowed to taste the product, I was so proud of what my dad had achieved.

"But what I walked in on, when I walked into his office, changed my opinion of my father and a whole load of other things." He swallowed, remembering that moment like it was five minutes ago, not almost twelve years. "I found him in a compromising position with a young woman who had just started working in the tasting room."

Bailey sighed, her tone soft. "Jeez, Quinn." The mask of fury she'd been wearing slipped a little. "Could you have mistaken what you saw?"

He shook his head. Since that day, he'd done everything he could to get the image out of his head of his dad taking his floozy from behind as she gripped the edges of his solid oak desk. But nothing had worked. He hadn't been mistaken.

"Until that moment," he continued, "I'd wanted nothing more than to be like my dad. To work in the distillery, meet a nice girl, get married and have a big, happy family. But everything changed that day. I didn't know what or who I could trust anymore. I hurt for Mom and wasn't sure whether to tell her or to keep it to myself. I knew one thing for certain. I never wanted to be like my dad and that meant making sure I never got involved in a committed relationship where I could be tempted to cheat."

It sounded a little stupid now he said it out loud, but his logic had worked for him for years. He'd been protecting himself and others.

"Did you ever tell your mom?" Bailey asked.

"No. Until today I haven't told a soul. I don't know if she knows—I don't think I want her to. Why spoil years of good memories? I don't think any of my brothers or sisters know, either. Dad saw me, though. He knew I knew, and he begged me not to say a word. He told me all men cheat and that monogamy is an unrealistic expectation put upon us by society." Quinn snorted. "He actually seemed kinda proud of what I'd seen."

Bailey raised her eyebrows. "Why'd you stick around?

I think if I'd seen something like that, I'd have left home and gone far, far away as soon as I could."

"I guess to protect Mom. To be there for her in case she ever found out. To help her keep up the pretense. And I like working at the distillery. I'm not sure what I'd do if I didn't do whiskey."

She shook her head, sadness showing in her eyes. He didn't know if she was shaking her head at the situation or the fact that once again he'd enabled a lie.

"He's the reason I've never committed to a woman. And that decision has been easy to adhere to until you. I promise, although I turned you away initially, I meant what I said about being unable to get you out of my head. I turned you away because, as you said, it was complicated because of your history with Callum, but also because I was scared of the intensity of my feelings. The sex we had was explosive, amazing, but I now realize the reason it was different from other times was because I was having it with you. I may have pursued you because of the babies—I admit, I didn't want my children to end up like Hallie and Hamish, torn between their parents— but you weren't the only one I fooled."

He swallowed as he tried to find the right words. "Somewhere over the last couple of months, I stopped *pretending* to want to be with you. If the joke's on anyone, it's me, because I've…I've fallen damn hard for you, Bailey Sawyer. I think I'm in love with you."

The moment the words escaped his mouth he knew they were the wrong ones. Dammit, he hadn't any practice at this.

Her eyes widened. "You *think*?" she spat.

"No, I know I'm in love with you. I've never felt this

way about anyone ever before and I know it's not going to change. Please, give me another chance."

Neither of them said anything for a few moments. Sweat pooled at the back of Quinn's neck as he waited for her to speak.

"They're just words, Quinn," she whispered, with an almost imperceptible shake of her head. "Nice words, but they're too easy to say and so much harder to believe under the circumstances. You might actually *think* you love me, but what happens when the buzz and shine of being new parents wears off?"

"It won't!" He yanked his hands out of his pockets and stepped toward her, reaching out and grabbing on to her arms. "I didn't believe in love, so I didn't recognize until we were right in the middle of it, but I promise you, what I feel for you is real."

Bailey shook her arms free of his grasp. "This is my mother and father all over again. Getting her pregnant with me made him think he loved her as well, but it wasn't enough. I'm sorry, Quinn, but I think it's best we stop pretending to each other. You are my babies' father and that won't ever change, but I think coparents is the only relationship we should have going forward."

Before he could argue, she added, "Now, if you don't mind, I really do need to get some sleep."

No! Every cell in his body wanted to grab hold of her and kiss some sense into her, but his head told him that wouldn't go down well. It might only further the chasm between them. As much as he hated to admit defeat, deep down he knew if he pushed too hard, he would only make things worse, and Bailey did need her sleep.

"Okay." He lowered his head in one slow nod. "But can I just ask you one favor before I go?"

"It's okay, Quinn, I promise I won't tell a soul about Aunt Bossy." She lifted her finger and moved it across her lips in a zipping action.

"That's not the favor." That hadn't even crossed his mind. Hell, he'd tell the world himself if that would make her believe his declaration. "Can you please not tell anyone, not even your mother, about my dad? I don't want to be the one to break Mom's heart."

"Of course. All your secrets are safe with me." And with that, she stepped past him and opened the front door, giving him the loud and clear message that this conversation was over.

Quinn had never felt more defeated in his life.

Chapter Twelve

Bailey sat in the waiting room of the ultrasound clinic, her knees chattering up and down.

"Are you okay, honey?" asked her mother. She put down the magazine she'd been flicking through and squeezed Bailey's knee.

What a complex question! Physically? Mentally? Emotionally? She was *not* okay in all of those areas to various degrees but was trying desperately not to let anyone know.

"I'm fine," she lied. "The babies are just making it difficult to get comfortable."

"Ah." Her mom nodded. "I remember when I was pregnant with you, Elle and Dane. Some days no matter what I did I couldn't get comfortable and I only had one baby at a time, but I promise you it'll all be worth it when you finally meet those two little people inside of you. Thanks so much for asking me to come with you today. I can't wait to see my grandbabies on the screen."

Bailey smiled in reply, trying to ignore the prick of remorse inside her at the thought that Quinn should be there instead of her mother. He'd been at every other scan so far, but she'd conveniently forgotten to tell him about this one.

In the last week, she'd become skilled in the art of avoiding him. She didn't answer his phone calls, and when he text messaged, she sent short replies and made excuses about being too busy at work to make time to meet and talk. What good would talking do anyway? He'd only try to convince her that his bogus feelings were real and she'd only end up getting angry, or worse, she might start to believe him.

Bailey wanted desperately to believe him and that was why she couldn't trust herself to be around him. She needed to be strong. For the sake of the babies… and her heart.

"Bailey Sawyer?"

The sound of her name drew her thoughts away from Quinn and she stood. "Come on, Mom."

The two of them hurried down the corridor and into the little room after the sonographer.

"Lovely to see you again, Bailey," Sherry said as she closed the door and gestured toward the examination table. Due to her need for frequent ultrasounds, Bailey felt as if she and Sherry were old friends and the routine of climbing onto the table and lifting her shirt was second nature.

"You, too." Bailey smiled. "This is my mom, Marcia Sawyer."

"Hi." Marcia offered her hand. "I'm very excited to be here."

"Hello, lovely to meet you." After greeting her mother, Sherry sat down on her stool and looked back to Bailey as she positioned herself on the table. "Is Quinn not coming today?"

"Um…he couldn't make it." Her cheeks heated with the little white lie and she didn't meet the eyes of either Sherry or her mother. Bailey had admitted to her mother that she and Quinn had decided to remove the romantic aspect of their relationship and focus on the more important things such as coparenting and friendship, but she hadn't confessed the whole sorry story. And she still hadn't worked out how she and Quinn were actually going to achieve these things when right now she couldn't stand to be in the same room as him, but she wasn't about to share her personal issues with a stranger.

"That's a pity. We'll have to be sure to get some good photos for him," Sherry said as she squeezed the gel onto Bailey's stomach, lifted the probe and began.

Bailey did her best to focus on the screen as that wonderful *thump-thump-thump* filled the room. Hearing her babies' hearts beat had become her favorite sound over the last few months, but it didn't give her quite the same buzz when Quinn wasn't there to share it. And she hated him for that. She hated that she couldn't win—whether he was here or not, either way she'd suffer.

"Is everything still looking good?" she asked, trying to forget about him.

Sherry moved the probe over her stomach. "Two healthy little fetuses. Twin one is slightly bigger this week than twin two, but unless things change dramatically in the next week, I don't think your doctor will be concerned."

"Oh, my goodness." Marcia bounced on her feet as she leaned over Bailey and pointed to the screen. "Is that what I think it is?"

Bailey scrutinized the screen to try to work out what her mom had seen as panic twisted in her gut. "Is something wrong?"

"No, nothing." Sherry looked over Bailey and gave her mother a pointed look. "Quinn and Bailey decided they didn't want to know the babies' sexes."

"Whoops." Marcia slapped her hand over her mouth but didn't keep it there very long. She glanced down at Bailey. "We don't have to tell anyone, but knowing you're having boys will make things a lot easier—we'll be able to buy clothes and organize the nursery properly now."

"Mom!" Bailey exclaimed, wishing she could un-hear what she'd just heard. She looked back to the image on the screen—the two black blobs were now clearly identifiable as babies, but at previous scans she and Quinn had been careful not to look too closely, since they'd agreed on wanting a surprise. Suddenly Bailey wasn't sure about that decision! Was it just another thing Quinn had fooled her into?

She looked uncertainly to Sherry. "Am I really having boys?"

"You sure you want to know?"

Bailey sighed, ignoring the prick of guilt inside her; her mom had pretty much ruined any chance of a surprise anyway. She nodded. "Yes, please."

Sherry moved the probe down lower on Bailey's belly and then pointed to the screen. "What do you think that is?"

It took a second, but then Bailey could clearly see what her mother had blurted. "Oh, my."

"Two little boys," Sherry said. "I bet Quinn will be stoked."

"You're going to have your hands full when they are little," Marcia patted Bailey's hand, "but I'll be here to help, and trust me, girls are painful when they hit puberty."

Bailey didn't think she'd ever been that much of a handful, but she buried her irritation with her mother as an image of two little boys who looked almost identical to Quinn landed in her head. They'd be gorgeous, without a doubt, but also a constant reminder for her broken heart about what she'd lost. Or rather, what she'd never really had.

Sherry completed the usual measurements and then gave Bailey some paper towels to wipe the gel from her belly. Once done, she retreated into the bathroom to relieve herself and contemplated messaging Quinn and telling him the news. Dammit. Although she'd inadvertently found out, doing so behind his back felt very, very wrong. Her gut rolled with guilt.

Bailey sat through her doctor's appointment barely taking in a word and then found herself agreeing to lunch with her mother, even though she wasn't hungry and wanted to escape and bury herself in work.

"You've got to eat," Marcia said in her I'm-going-to-win-so-you-might-as-well-give-in-anyway tone.

Somehow lunch turned into her mom dragging her into a nearby department store. Bailey glanced around, relieved to see no one she knew, as Marcia strolled into the baby-clothes section.

"Oh, would you look at these." Her mother grabbed a little outfit of tiny navy jeans and a red flannel cowboy shirt off the rack. She held it up and then grabbed another with a blue shirt. "I just have to buy these. The twins are going to look gorgeous in them."

Bailey summoned a smile, wishing she could catch some of her mom's enthusiasm. What could possibly be more exciting than buying baby clothes? They were just the cutest darn things in the world. But she couldn't get over the culpability she felt about finding out the babies' sexes behind Quinn's back.

"Hey, Bailey. Hi, Marcia."

She spun around at the voice to see Quinn's sister Annabel standing only a few feet away. "Hi. What are you doing here?" The question sounded a lot more accusing than she'd meant it to.

Seemingly unaware or unperturbed, Annabel shrugged one shoulder. "One of the guys at the firehouse just had a baby and we're putting money in to buy him and his wife a present. As I'm the token female there, the task fell to me. Honestly, for a supposedly modern world, I sometimes feel like we're still stuck in the dark ages. What do I know about buying baby stuff?"

Bailey laughed nervously and tried to sneakily glare at her mother to put the little cowboy outfits back. Of course, she didn't take the hint.

"They are so adorable," Annabel said, reaching out and touching her finger to the red shirt. "Pity you don't know what you're having."

Bailey swallowed, her chest tightened and she wished she could turn back time. She'd always been a shocking liar. She could have just nodded—Annabel had made a statement, not asked a question—but instead Bailey found herself blurting out the truth. "I just found out. Two boys."

"Oh." Annabel's friendly smile vanished. "Does Quinn know?"

While the McKinnels had always liked her, always made her feel like one of the clan, Bailey knew that if they ever had to make a choice, they'd side with family. Blood thicker than water and all that.

"No," she admitted, biting down on the urge to try to explain herself, because she didn't have any reasonable excuse. If she'd told him about the date change in their appointment, he would have been there instead of her mother. He was going to be pissed and she couldn't blame him.

"I see. Well, I guess you'll be telling him very soon," Annabel said, and it was clear that if Bailey didn't, she would.

"Yes. Of course." She nodded so hard she gave herself a headache, or maybe that was down to the whole messy situation.

"Good. Well." Annabel looked around the baby department. "I guess I'd better go pick out this present and get back to the firehouse. See ya."

"Okay. Bye." Annabel had disappeared into the next aisle barely before Bailey managed to utter those words. She wondered how long it would take for her to message Quinn.

She turned to tell her mom she was done with shopping and didn't want lunch, only to find her already over at the counter, laughing with the sales assistant as she paid for the two little cowboy outfits.

"They're for my new grandsons," she heard Marcia announce. "My daughter is having twins and we just found out they're boys!"

Bailey rolled her eyes, realizing that before she went

back to work, she had to call Quinn, because even if Annabel didn't spill the news, this was yet another secret her mom wasn't going to be able to keep.

Quinn marched into the staff room at the distillery and headed straight for the fridge. He yanked it open and stared inside, looking for something—anything—that would make him feel better. He was grumpy and hungry, and while he couldn't seem to do anything about the first problem, he thought maybe he could fix the latter. But he hadn't brought anything in for lunch and it looked like Sophie hadn't stocked the fridge with yummy snacks as she sometimes did. He slammed it shut again and thumped the side of the refrigerator.

"So, I guess it's true you and Bailey have split?" said Mac from behind him.

Quinn had barely registered his brother sitting at the table devouring a sandwich. "I'm just hungry," he growled, eyeing the other half of Mac's lunch on his plate. He'd never been through a proper breakup before, and if this was how it felt, then he never wanted to do so again.

"Right." Mac's tone said he didn't buy that excuse for a moment. He pushed his plate toward Quinn. "Sounds like you need it more than me."

Quinn pulled out a chair, sat and lifted the sandwich to his mouth. He gobbled it down in a few quick bites and then sat there in silence, waiting for the food hit to lift his mood.

Quinn looked to his brother. "You've been in love before, right?"

Mac lifted one eyebrow. "So you *want* to talk about Bailey now?"

"It's a pain in the ass, right?"

"What? Love or women?"

"Both."

Mac chuckled. "What happened between you two? You were all gooey-eyed and lovey-dovey leading up to Mom's party, and then suddenly it's over?"

Quinn sighed and ran a hand through his hair. "It's kinda a long story."

Mac leaned back in his seat and linked his hands behind his head. "I'm kinda my own boss, so I kinda have all day."

Although neither of them had ever been big talkers in the past—preferring to kick a ball around or share a few drinks when it came to brotherly bonding—Quinn found himself spilling his guts. Everything from the crush he'd always harbored on Bailey, to comforting her when she was questioning her relationship with Callum, to finding out about her pregnancy in the inauspicious manner that he had.

"And I get that she's pissed," he said, "but I don't know what else to do. She refuses to see me. She won't even answer my calls. I don't know how to convince her that my feelings, my...*love* is real." He still found the *L* word a little awkward to roll off the tongue, especially when conversing with his brother, but a week apart from Bailey had only convinced him further of his feelings.

"Wait!" Mac held up a hand and leaned forward. "Let me get this straight. *You* are the infamous Aunt Bossy?" Before Quinn could answer, Mac broke out in loud, uncontrolled laughter.

With a roll of his eyes, Quinn shoved back his chair. "If you're just gonna be an asshole about it, I'm outta here."

He didn't know why he'd thought confiding in one of

his brothers was a good idea, especially Mac, whose track record with love wasn't that much better than his own. Perhaps he should consult an advice columnist himself. What guidance would he offer to someone if a letter arrived from a man in his current situation who wanted to know what he needed to do to make things right? Fact was, most of his letters were from women—men, by nature, didn't ask for help—and if he had any idea what to suggest, he'd have already tried it.

"I'm sorry," Mac called when Quinn was almost at the staff room door. "Look, I don't have any answers for you, but how about you come help me knock down a wall in the old café? I find demolition always makes me feel better."

Quinn paused. He wasn't sure anything would lift his mood right now, but Mac's suggestion beat hanging around in the warehouse feeling sorry for himself. "I could probably spare a couple of hours if you need my help."

Mac shrugged. "The job will get done faster and that will keep the big boss happy."

The big boss, aka Callum, hadn't stopped smiling in days. Quinn reckoned they could set fire to the whole distillery and he'd still be happy. He tried not to begrudge Callum and Chelsea their fairy tale, but he couldn't help feeling a little bitter.

"Let's do it," he said. "And do you mind keeping the Aunt Bossy thing to yourself?"

Mac slid his finger across his lips. "I won't tell a soul."

They'd had to close the café to complete the extension and Callum wanted it done ASAP so they could get back to the important task of making money.

Half an hour later, as Quinn slammed a sledgehammer against the wall and watched the drywall crumble, he had to admit the physical labor made him feel a darn sight better than talking and thinking. *Thwump, thwump, thwump*—with each swing of his sledgehammer, he felt a tiny bit of tension inside him easing. The only thing that might work even better was sex, and unfortunately that was a no-go zone right now, because if he couldn't have it with Bailey, he didn't want to have it with anyone else.

This in itself should prove his love because he'd sure as hell never been this discriminating before.

"Thanks for asking me to help," Quinn said, once he and Mac stepped back to take a look at what they'd achieved.

Mac nodded his head once. "You're the one doing me a favor. The faster I finish this, the quicker I can get on with the next job."

"Next job?"

"Yep. Claire's parents want me to add a games room to their place."

"So, this is what you're going to do now?" Quinn asked, gesturing to the rubble around them. "Build stuff?" While Mac was undoubtedly good at construction, it was hard to imagine him giving up soccer for good.

Mac scowled as if he didn't want to answer that question, and at the same time, Quinn's cell rang in his pocket. Wiping sweat from his forehead with the back of his hand, he dug the phone out with his other hand and almost leaped into the air when he saw the caller was Bailey. He swallowed and then looked to Mac. "It's her," he hissed, staring down at his phone as if it might spontaneously combust at any moment.

Mac nodded toward the cell. "I thought you wanted to talk to her?"

"I did. I *do*."

"Well then, answer the freaking thing," Mac suggested, before turning and walking through the wall they'd just decimated.

"Good plan," Quinn muttered. He slid his finger across the screen to answer and then lifted the phone to his ear. "Bailey."

"Hi, Quinn."

It was *so* good to hear her voice, but silence followed for a few moments, as if neither of them had any idea what to say next. Until a week ago, they'd spoken at least twice a day on the phone and had never been hard-pushed to find anything to say to each other. Now he didn't want to speak for fear of saying the wrong thing.

"I've been trying to call you for over an hour," Bailey said. She didn't sound happy about this fact and he swallowed the urge to mention all his calls she'd been ignoring.

"I'm sorry. I didn't hear the phone. I've been knocking down a wall in the café with Mac."

"So you haven't spoken to Annabel yet?"

"No." Quinn frowned, wondering what his sister had to do with anything. "Why?"

Silence followed, which Quinn desperately wanted to fill, but he didn't want to risk upsetting or annoying her. It felt like forever before she finally said, "I had an ultrasound today."

Something squeezed inside him, like a hand curling around his gut. "I thought our appointment was tomorrow." He'd been looking forward to it, not simply to see his babies again, but because she wouldn't be able to ignore him when they were face-to-face.

"They moved it forward a day."

Quinn's first instinct was to demand why she hadn't told him, but he pushed it aside and asked the more important question. The question that made his heart stop beating. "Is something wrong with the babies?"

"No," she rushed to assure him. "Nothing like that."

Relief washed over him, but he could tell this wasn't a social call. His patience waning, he asked, "What is it, then?"

"I'm sorry, Quinn, but I found out the babies' sexes today."

It took a moment for this news to register, but then, "What the hell?"

It was bad enough her not telling him about the changed appointment, but then going against what they'd decided together? That hurt like nothing had before. And he guessed that had been her agenda—to hurt him like he'd hurt her—but no way was he going to let her cut him out of the babies' lives. She couldn't just go making decisions that affected them without him.

"It wasn't a conscious decision. Mom took one look at the screen and could tell. I *said* I'm sorry." She sounded more defensive than sorry, and that only got his back up more. He wasn't sure whether he believed the story about Marcia, either.

"What was Marcia doing there? I'm the one that should have been there, dammit. I won't let you shut me out like this." His grip tightened on his cell. "They're my babies as well, even if you wish they weren't."

"I know that," she snapped, "but don't take that tone

with me. You're not the boss of me and you don't get to tell me what I can and can't do."

"Maybe not," he reluctantly agreed, "but this is exactly what I didn't want for our kids—parents who can't agree or speak to each other without raising their voices."

"You're the one yelling at me!"

"I'm sorry." Quinn closed his eyes and silently counted to ten. In all the time he'd known Bailey, she'd never been this unreasonable. They needed to stop acting like bickering schoolkids and start acting like responsible parents. "We both need to calm down and make a time to meet and talk about all of this. About how we are going to navigate the road ahead. I don't want to be a part-time dad. Can you do dinner tonight?"

She hesitated a moment and he prayed for a positive answer. Yes, they needed to talk, but he also *needed* to see her. He missed her. Living by himself had always been a joy, but the past week of going to bed and waking up alone had been anything but. He missed holding her. He missed asking her about her day and telling her about his.

"I'm really busy at work this week and too tired to go out in the evenings," she said. "We still have a few more months to work out the logistics, so there's no huge rush. Let's go for a coffee or something after next week's ultrasound and talk then."

Next week? She may as well have suggested they meet next century. How could he prove how he felt if she wouldn't even give him a chance? Yet, short of barging over to her place and forcing his way inside—which might only alienate her further—what else could he do but acquiesce? Perhaps if she saw he thought her worth holding out for, she would finally believe and accept his love.

"Okay. But if you change your mind and want to talk before then, call me. Anytime, day or night."

"I'll see you next week, Quinn."

"Wait!" He raised his voice, hoping she hadn't disconnected. "You didn't say. Are we buying pink or blue clothes?"

She made a *tsk* sound between her teeth. "Such notions of gender are ridiculous and outdated. Real men aren't afraid to wear pink and girls can sure as heck wear blue."

Oh, for... Could he say nothing right?

Before he could defend himself, she added, "But if you mean what sex are the twins, then we're having boys."

Boys. For the first time in a week Quinn truly smiled. Girls would have been just as good. He'd meant it when he'd said he didn't care what they were as long as they were healthy, but he understood guys, whereas he sure didn't understand women right now.

"That's awesome," he said. "At least now we can narrow down the names."

But all he got in reply was three little beeps telling him Bailey had already disconnected the phone.

Chapter Thirteen

It felt like Groundhog Day to Bailey as she walked toward the clinic for her weekly scan. The only difference was that previously she'd always been excited—unable to wait to see how much the twins had grown, to hear that beautiful synchronized beat of their hearts. Today her own heart danced with trepidation at the prospect of seeing Quinn again after a two-week drought.

She paused in front of the building, deliberating whether to go in or wait for him outside. Could he already be in there, or would he wait for her if he got there first? Unsure of the answer, she glanced left and then right and saw him striding toward her, his long legs gobbling up the sidewalk between them. Her stomach did a traitorous flip as she drank Quinn in—he wore smart but faded jeans and a McKinnel's Distillery polo-neck shirt, as if he'd come from work. And, unless she was seeing things, he looked even more gorgeous than she recalled.

He offered her a tentative smile as he stopped a few feet in front of her. Awkwardness filled the space between them. In the past, when they were just friends, he'd have kissed her cheek in a friendly, familiar greeting. Only a couple of weeks ago, he'd have pulled her into his arms and locked his lips with hers, sparking shivers of awareness all over her body.

But things had changed. Not the reaction of her body, but…

"Hi, Bailey," he said, his voice low. Those two words sounded so loaded the hairs on her arms stood to attention.

"Hi." As much as she hated to admit it, it felt good to see him. So many times over the last week, she'd almost picked up the phone and called him, but common sense had gotten the better of her every single time. They needed to set up boundaries. She needed to keep a wall around her to protect her heart.

"Shall we go in?" He gestured to the door behind them.

She nodded and he stepped past her, holding it open for her as he might do for any old stranger, no touching the small of her back as he'd done on previous occasions. Bailey felt both relieved and disappointed about this and wished her thoughts would stop being so contrary. As was their routine, Quinn went and sat in the row of plastic chairs and she went over to the reception desk to register their arrival.

"We're running a little late today," apologized the lady behind the desk. "You'll have to wait about half an hour."

"Okay." Bailey smiled and nodded, when in reality she wanted to lean over the desk, grab this woman by her collar and demand they go in right this second. Her bladder would burst within the next thirty minutes, but more important, she would have to sit alongside Quinn, breathing in his intoxicating scent and making conversation, while they waited.

He looked up from the sports magazine he'd been flicking through as she approached.

"They're behind schedule," she said as she tried to work out where to park herself. Only the seats on either side of him were free, so she didn't have much choice unless she wanted to sit on the other side of the room. That would be childish.

"Are you alright?" he asked as she lowered herself into the seat on his left. Getting up and down became more of a challenge every day. He placed a steadying palm on her arm and she startled as if he'd struck her with a match.

"Sorry." He held up his hands and leaned back in his seat.

"I'm fine," she said through gritted teeth as she folded her hands on her belly and tried to relax.

They sat in awkward silence for what felt like an eternity, but the clock above the reception desk told her only eight and a half minutes had passed. Bailey tried to think of everything *but* Quinn and her bladder; failing dismally on both accounts.

He was the first to break the silence. "How've you been the last couple of weeks?"

How had she been? What kind of dumb-ass question was that?

Truth was, she hadn't been feeling the best over the last few days—she'd experienced a little tightening and a slight pain in her abdomen and hoped it wasn't a sign of early labor—but she wasn't going to tell him that. She put it down to stress—caused by him. "Much the same as any woman twenty-two weeks pregnant with twins who works full-time would feel, I imagine."

"You know you don't have to work full-time," he said. "We'll need to work out some kind of child support payments when the twins are born, and I don't mind helping you out before then, either."

"Maybe I want to work," she snapped. "It keeps my mind off other things."

Quinn inhaled and exhaled loudly as if losing his patience with her. "Of course, whatever you want. I just wanted you to know the option is there. I'm here to help in any way you need."

When their usual sonographer came out into the waiting room, Bailey's heart leaped, but Sherry called out another name, and another couple—who looked nauseatingly happy together—stood and followed her.

"While we're waiting, we may as well start talking about what we're going to do when the twins are born," Quinn said. "Discuss possible custody arrangements."

The phrase *custody arrangements* made her skin crawl. "Obviously I'll have full custody for at least the first year while they're nursing. After that…" Her voice trailed off. She didn't want to think about after that. She hadn't even met the twins and already she couldn't bear the thought of being separated from them while they went to their father. Tears prickled at the corner of her eyes.

"No."

It took a second for Quinn's one word to register. She turned her head to glare at him. "What do you mean *no*?"

"I'm a big supporter of breast-feeding, and if that all works out well, then of course I want our boys to get what's best, but that doesn't mean I'm not going to be there to help with the burping and diaper changing, or to give you a break when you need one. So, either I move in with you, or you move in with me for the first year of their lives."

What the heck? She was about to ask this question when a man called, "Miss Sawyer?"

"That's us," Quinn said, standing and offering her his hand. Befuddled, she took it without thinking, a jolt of awareness shooting up her arm as he assisted her out of the seat.

Annoyed at herself as much as at him, she snatched her hand from his and followed the man down the corridor and into one of the rooms.

"Hi," he said, offering his hand first to Bailey and then to Quinn. "I'm Cameron, one of the sonographers here. I see you've been coming for regular scans, so it's a surprise we haven't met yet."

"Nice to meet you." Quinn shook the other man's hand. "This is Bailey and I'm Quinn."

"I guess you guys know the drill," Cameron said, gesturing for Bailey to climb up on the table.

She did so, feeling strangely unsettled.

Cameron wasn't as chatty as Sherry and he got straight down to business. Within a few seconds of his smearing the gel on her swollen belly, Bailey heard the *thump-thump-thump* of her babies' hearts and some of her anxiety lifted a little.

"Is it just me or is one baby bigger than the other?" Quinn leaned toward her as he peered over her at the computer screen. While her hormones inhaled deeply like wanton hussies, she tried to be annoyed by this invasion of personal space.

The sonographer gave a clearly awkward smile and nodded. "Yes, very astute. We have seen a significant growth in one fetus over the last week and none in the other. I'm going to see if there's a doctor available. Back in a moment."

As Cameron put the probe back in its holder and started out of the room, Bailey snapped her head to look at Quinn. His usually smooth brow was creased as his gaze met hers. Suddenly she found it difficult to breathe. Was something wrong with one of the twins?

"They…were…fine…last week," she managed, too scared to even cry.

"It'll be alright." He leaned toward her, wrapped his arm around her and drew her into his warm body. His other hand took hold of hers and squeezed. "Let's not jump to conclusions."

They didn't speak as they waited, but Bailey couldn't be disappointed that Quinn was here. She ignored the voice inside her that told her *not* to accept his comfort and support, because right now he was the only person in the world who could have any idea how scared she felt. She'd seen the terror in his face, too.

After what seemed like an eternity, Cameron returned with Doctor Mackie, her ob-gyn, whom she'd been seeing monthly, and Bailey could have kissed him. How lucky that her own doctor just happened to be on duty.

"Hi, Bailey. Hi, Quinn," the doctor said as he picked up the ultrasound probe. "Do you mind if I take a little look?" It was a rhetorical question, and neither Bailey nor Quinn said anything as he squeezed on more gel and then pressed the probe against her belly.

As he examined her, his eyes narrowed and he scrutinized the images on the screen. Bailey held her breath and clung to Quinn's hand as if it were a lifeline, trying to read the expression on the doctor's face.

Finally, he spoke. "I'm sorry to say that it looks like your fetuses are suffering from twin-to-twin transfusion syndrome."

Quinn's grip on her hand tightened.

"But they were fine last week," she protested, not wanting to hear another word of what could only be bad news. She didn't need to ask what this meant, they'd been warned that sometimes, in the case of identical twins who shared the same placenta, there was an unequal flow of blood between the fetuses, causing one twin to thrive while the other did not.

Dr. Mackie bowed his head. "With monochorionic twins the in-utero situation can change quickly, and issues with the placenta are always a possibility. That's why you've been having weekly scans." He pointed to the screen at what Bailey could now clearly see was the smaller twin. Her stomach clenched. "See how twin one has a lot more amniotic fluid around him than twin two? Everything I'm seeing indicates that you are in stage one TTTS."

"So what exactly does this mean for Bailey and our babies?" Quinn asked, the confidence he usually spoke with noticeably absent.

"I'm going to urgently refer you to Doctor Linda Kowalski, a specialist who deals with TTTS. She will discuss your options going forward and talk about the possibility of placental laser surgery if things continue to head in this direction."

Quinn nodded. "Thank you. And in the meantime, is there anything Bailey should or shouldn't do to help the situation? Anything *I* can do to help?"

She was glad Quinn asked because the lump that had formed in her throat made it impossible for her to speak.

Dr. Mackie offered her a paper towel to wipe her belly, before straightening and clearing his throat. "I don't want you to stress too much at this stage. Dr. Kowalski will provide a care plan going forward, but I'd advise continuing to eat nutritiously, especially foods high in protein, and getting plenty of liquids and bed rest." He looked to Quinn and winked. "If Bailey is feeling amorous, there's no need to abstain, but I'd suggest she takes the reins and goes on top, so as not to put too much pressure on the cervix. But if Mom's feeling good, the babies will, as well."

Oh. My. Lord. She guessed the doctor was merely trying to lighten things up a little, but thinking about sex with Quinn was the last thing she needed right now. Her cheeks scorching, she couldn't look any of the men in the room in the eye, least of all him.

"Can I go to the bathroom?" she blurted, extracting her hand from his.

"Of course." Dr. Mackie smiled as he stepped back to give her room to climb off the table. "I'll write your referral and pass it on to Quinn. See you soon."

Bailey couldn't get out of the room fast enough. She closed the bathroom door behind her and the tears she'd been too shocked to cry until now tumbled free and down her cheeks. Letting them fall, she sat there and hugged her arms around her belly, the fear for the tiny lives inside her squeezing the breath from her lungs.

What else did life want to throw at her?

She would do anything right now if it allowed both her babies to thrive—but what could she do? The feeling of being utterly powerless was like no devastation she'd ever felt before.

A while later, she couldn't be sure how long, the doors

to the restrooms opened and Quinn's voice immediately followed. "Bails, are you in there?"

She opened her mouth to call out, to tell him to leave, but only a guttural sob escaped. Two seconds later his head appeared over the cubicle door. Instead of freaking out about him seeing her in such a state, she welcomed the sight of him.

Her eyes locked with his. "I'm scared, Quinn."

Standing on tippy-toes, Quinn looked down over the top of the cubicle door at Bailey and swallowed. Was this his fault? Had the stress she'd been under these last couple of weeks somehow triggered this?

"That's understandable," he said, trying to contain his own emotion. He needed to be strong for her. "But at least they've picked it up early. Dr. Kowalski sounds like she will know what to do. I'm sure it'll be okay. Come on, open the door."

She nodded slowly and Quinn stepped back, giving her a moment to pull herself together. Well aware he shouldn't be in the women's restroom, he didn't retreat but instead waited while Bailey flushed the toilet and unlocked the door. He wasn't about to leave her alone again. She stepped out, hitched her purse up on her shoulder and looked to him, her eyes red with thick black around them where her mascara had run. Her cheeks were blotchy and damp.

He resisted the urge to pull her into his arms—he didn't want her to accuse him of taking advantage of their awful situation, although he did hope that maybe their shared concern would somehow bring them closer together. "Come on. Let's get you out of here."

"I just need to wash my hands." She sniffed, stepped

up to the vanity and glanced into the mirror as she turned on the taps. "God, what a sight!"

He swallowed. What was the right thing to say in this situation? He honestly thought her gorgeous, even in this forlorn and helpless state, but saying anything of the sort might sound like a come-on. He'd seen her horror when Dr. Mackie had mentioned sex and he didn't want to upset her any further. Perhaps it was best to not say anything at all.

"Would you like me to wait outside for you?" he asked.

She met his gaze in the mirror and nodded. "Thank you. I won't be a moment."

At least she hadn't told him to get lost, he thought as he opened the door and stepped into the corridor. He wanted to be there for her—he wanted them to be there for each other—but it was so hard to know how to navigate such a thing when their last few conversations had been like battles between warring countries.

After a few more moments of tapping his feet, Bailey appeared. "Thanks for waiting," she said, obviously trying to sound strong and collected. Although she'd clearly washed her face and reapplied her makeup, she couldn't hide her vulnerability from him. She lifted a hand to push some hair back out her eye and he noticed her hand shaking.

No way could he let her drive home in this agitated state. They'd intended to go to a café to talk about the future, but the logistics of how they would parent didn't seem as pressing right now. All he wanted was to see her home safely. To make sure she did as she was told and got some rest.

"Let me drive you home," he said, expecting her to object. When she simply nodded, he took her hand and started toward the clinic exit. "I'll have Mac come pick me up from your place and collect my car later."

Whether she heard or not, she didn't comment, and she didn't yank her hand from his, either, which just went to show how worried she was. He didn't want to take advantage of this situation, but he couldn't help enjoying the feel of her hand in his once again. The word *right* came to mind, and he knew he had to do whatever it took to get her to see that they were supposed to be together. As a couple. As a family.

"Where are you parked?" he asked as they emerged onto the street.

"Just round the corner." She dug her keys out of her purse and handed them to him. "I feel stupid letting you drive, but I'm feeling a little distracted. Are you sure *you're* okay to drive?"

"Yes. I'm fine. Don't get me wrong, the news of the TTTS scares the bejeesus out of me, but I'm not the one carrying the babies."

"I'm sorry." Her words came out on another sob. "My stupid body is failing them."

"That is not true," he said, coming to a halt and turning her to face him. Without thinking, he put his hand against her cheek and forced her to look into his eyes as he spoke. "This is *not* your fault. You can't think like that. We need to stay positive, for the twins."

"I know," she whispered, her eyes watering once again. "I just wish there was something I could do. They're my babies. I'm supposed to be able to look after them."

Her babies, her responsibility—her words killed him, but he wasn't about to get in an argument right now.

"Then let's get you home and resting. Come on." He dropped his hand and continued to walk alongside her, mourning the loss of body contact but unable to touch her with the knowledge that she was only letting him do so because she was in a vulnerable state.

They reached the car and he helped her into her seat, then jogged round and climbed in himself. He turned the key in the ignition and the sultry sounds of a local band drifted out of the radio. Bailey barely seemed to notice, and although the music wasn't to Quinn's usual taste, at least it filled what would otherwise likely be awkward silence. He'd wanted more than anything to spend some time alone with her again, but he hadn't wished it to be like this.

Fate could be a cruel bastard sometimes.

It seemed to take forever to get back to Jewell Rock, and when he pulled into her apartment's parking lot, she turned and hit him with her magic smile, but the light in her eyes wasn't as strong as usual. "Do you mind coming in for a bit?" She paused and rubbed her lips one over the other. "I don't really feel like being alone right now."

"Of course." He'd make her a hot chocolate and something to eat, get her settled in front of a feel-good movie and then retreat to a dark corner to digest this terrifying news.

"Thank you."

They walked solemnly to her front door.

"You've got my keys," she said.

"Oh, right." He dug them out of his pocket where he'd put them without thinking and handed them over. Their fingers brushed against each other in the exchange and every muscle in his body felt the effect. Their gazes met and the air between them buzzed with awareness. Keeping his hands to himself where Bailey was concerned felt like torture.

He swallowed, and just as he was about to force himself to break the moment, she leaned forward, stretched up and did the last thing he expected.

She kissed him.

Hallelujah! screamed his libido. It would be so easy to succumb to Bailey's lips, lift his hands to her breasts and get lost in the moment, but she wasn't in the right frame of mind. Again, he remembered her look of horror when their doctor had mentioned intimacy.

Summoning every inch of willpower he possessed, he tore his mouth from hers and took a step back, holding his hands out and putting distance between them. "You don't want to do that," he said.

Her eyes wide, she nodded, then reached out, grabbed a chunk of his shirt and tried to pull him back toward her. "Yes, I do," she said. "I just want to feel something other than anxiety for the twins for a few moments. *Please*, Quinn. Come inside and distract me. You heard what Dr. Mackie said—this won't hurt them. And I *need* it."

But what about me? While his body was one hundred percent behind this plan to distract their heads from the pain and worry, he wasn't going to get physical with her unless she was offering more than just sex. He wanted more from life, more from Bailey, more for himself.

He would do almost anything for this woman, but he wouldn't do that. He wouldn't allow Bailey to use him for his body, for oblivion, and then toss him to the curb again. He wasn't going to be something she regretted ever again.

"No." Quinn shook his head and shoved his hands in his pockets, refusing to succumb to her tempting offer. He knew that if she'd been thinking straight, she would not have propositioned him and that knowledge gave him the strength to resist.

"No?" Bailey blinked and shook her head slightly, her shock at his refusing sex obvious. "What? Am I not attractive enough for you now? Come on, Quinn, we both know you're not that choosy. I *need* this."

Her words wounded like no physical assault ever had—she might be emotional and not in the right frame of mind, but still her low opinion of him hurt like hell.

"I think you're the sexiest woman alive—you could be covered in mud and wearing trash bags, and I'd still want to be with you, but unless *you* can tell me you won't regret this tomorrow, I can't do it. I love you, Bailey Sawyer. I had never told any woman I love her until I told you. I did not say it lightly or because I thought it was what you wanted to hear, and it kills me that you don't believe me. But I won't make *love* to you unless you believe in us as much as I do." He paused, then asked, "Do you believe, Bailey?"

She glanced down at the ground, and when she looked back up after a few long moments, he could see her answer. "I want to…"

The *but* hung unspoken in the air like a knife twisting in his heart.

"I've made plenty of mistakes where you're concerned," he told her, already retreating, "and this isn't going to be another one."

Walking away from Bailey—even though Quinn knew it to be the right thing—wasn't getting any easier to do. He walked fast, fearful that if he slowed down he might lose his resolve and go back. His libido definitely wanted him to.

As he rounded the parking lot he remembered he'd left his transport in Bend.

He kicked the cement beneath his feet and ran a hand through his hair. The last thing he felt like doing right now was calling Mac to come pick him up and having to answer his inevitable questions, so he started to jog in the direction of home. He could worry about his SUV tomorrow and hopefully the physical exertion would help him de-stress a little.

He was halfway there when a vehicle slowed alongside him; he didn't look up but just kept on pounding the sidewalk.

"When did you take up jogging?" Annabel called, and Quinn cursed his bad luck. Of all the people who could have been driving past, it had to be a member of his family.

"About two minutes ago," he called back, without slowing.

"Can I suggest you buy a better pair of shoes and maybe some shorts? In my experience, jogging in jeans is always tricky."

The words *can I suggest you leave me the hell alone* were on the tip of his tongue, but he swallowed them. She was right—he wasn't dressed for exercise and he did need to collect his car. He slowed to a stop and walked over to her.

"Where are you off to?" he asked, resting his hands on the open window.

"Just coming home from work. What about you?"

He opened the passenger-side door and climbed in. "It's a long, boring story, which ends with me needing to collect my car from Bend. Want to give me a lift, little sis?"

She sighed. "Sadly, that is the best offer I've had all day." Then she turned the car back onto the road. "Hey, wasn't Bailey's ultrasound today? How was it?"

Quinn swallowed and shifted in his seat. "Not that great, actually. The scan showed that one of the babies isn't growing as well as the other. They think they're suffering from something called twin-to-twin transfusion syndrome."

"That doesn't sound good. What does it mean?"

He explained as much as he knew, unable to keep the tremor out of his voice.

"So one baby is taking nutrients from the other?" Annabel said. "Sibling rivalry already."

He knew she was trying to make him feel better, but he wasn't in the mood for lighthearted quips.

"What can they do about this transfusion thing?" she asked after a few moments of silence.

"We're going to see a doctor who specializes in TTTS, so we'll know more about it soon. Bailey's ob-gyn thinks she's only in stage one of the syndrome, but we're going to see a specialist to manage it."

"Is it dangerous?

"It can be," Quinn said, his chest squeezing again at the thought of anything happening to Bailey or the babies.

"How's she handling it?"

He thought of the way she'd thrown herself at him less than half an hour ago. "Not that great."

Annabel glanced his way and frowned. "Then why aren't you with her? Taking care of her?"

His fingers curled, making his hands into fists. "You don't think that's where I want to be? This is tearing me apart as well, but Bailey won't let me close." Well, not in the way he wanted her to. "She doesn't want anything to do with me."

"And how do you feel about her?" Annabel spoke calmly as if she were asking about the weather, not about his whole world.

"I love her, dammit."

Annabel grinned as if she was very much enjoying this conversation. "And I assume you've told her this."

"Of course I have, but she doesn't believe me. She thinks I'm only with her because of the babies."

"So what are you going to do about that?" she asked.

"What *can* I do about it? If you have any smart ideas, I'm all ears."

"You have to prove it to her. Do something she'd never expect you to do to show your love."

"Like what?"

She shrugged. "I'm a firefighter, not a love doctor. That, my dear brother, is up to you to work out."

Chapter Fourteen

Bailey's whole body burned, from her toenails to the tips of her ears, as Quinn stormed off. He couldn't get away from her fast enough. Her chest heaved and her lips buzzed from their brush with his only moments before. She must look even worse than she thought for *him* to turn down the opportunity of a quickie!

Fumbling to get the key in her door, she pushed it open, not wanting to risk one of her neighbors coming along and seeing her in this mortifying state. She stepped inside, slammed the door behind her and then leaned back against it, her heart still hammering. Had he really just brushed her off? He, who'd been more than happy to oblige the last time she'd needed to forget about her problems. And that was all she wanted now—a few moments to focus on something else.

Was he punishing her? Was not taking her to bed payback for all the things she'd done to him? For dithering over telling him about her pregnancy, for ruining his favorite jacket, for finding out about the babies' sexes behind his back? She hurled her keys across the hallway, which knocked a vase off the side table. As it crashed to the floor and broke into a zillion pieces, she cursed Quinn's name.

Because of him, she would be alone tonight, with nothing to do but worry about twin-to-twin transfusion syndrome. As a sob escaped her mouth, she bent down to pick up the big pieces of glass. After struggling to get up, she went into the kitchen, dumped them there and glanced around for her dustpan and brush to clean the rest of the mess. Her gaze caught on the glass Quinn had used that night he'd made her a milk shake and propositioned her about his Mom's party. The first of his many, many lies.

Her thumb throbbing, she glanced down and noticed she'd cut herself on the vase. Dammit, she shoved her bleeding thumb into her mouth and went into the bathroom to get a Band-Aid. As she retrieved her little first aid kid, she was struck with déjà vu. The last time she'd been tending to a cut it had been Quinn's finger that was bleeding. Her stomach tightened at the recollection.

Everything was a memory of him. And no matter how hard she'd tried to forget these last couple of weeks, she couldn't erase his declaration of love from her head.

He was a charmer alright, she thought as she wrapped a plaster around her thumb just a little too tightly.

The way he bandied around the L-O-V-E word, trying to manipulate her into doing parenthood his way, made her sick. She knew that not sleeping with her was simply another form of controlling her. But as mortifying as what had just happened was, it was a good thing he'd turned her down. Imagine if she'd let him into her bed, into her body and into her heart again. She was a fool to think she could sleep with him and keep her emotions separate.

With that thought, Bailey went into her bedroom and crawled into bed, trying not to think about how large and empty it felt without him in it. She knew she needed to eat for the babies' sake, but right now she just wanted to rest. The stress of the afternoon had compounded her tiredness—maybe if she just had a little nap, she'd wake up with a clearer head, be able to feed herself and then maybe even send Quinn a quick message apologizing for overstepping the boundaries *she'd* instigated.

Bailey awoke to the buzzing of her mobile on her bedside table. As she rolled over and stretched to pick it up, she frowned at the bright sun blaring in through her curtains. When she'd climbed into bed, it had been heading towards dusk and…

Good grief, how long have I slept?

Seeing her mom's name on caller ID, she sighed and put the phone back down. It stopped ringing, only to strike up again a few seconds later. She groaned, not in the mood to talk to her mother, but knowing that if she didn't pick up, Marcia would keep on calling, or worse, come over and let herself into the apartment with the spare key Bailey had stupidly given her.

Reluctantly she answered the call and lifted the phone to her ear. "Hi, Mom."

"Did you know about Quinn?" Marcia demanded.

Bailey blinked, still half-asleep. "What about him?" And then she realized she must have heard wrong and that Quinn must have told his mom about the TTTS and

Nora had told Marcia. As upset as she'd been last night, she hadn't even thought to call and tell her herself.

"That he's Aunt Bossy—you know, the newspaper advice columnist? *She's* Quinn McKinnel."

"What?" Bailey sat up in bed, suddenly wide-awake. "How do *you* know that?" He'd sworn she was the only person aside from him and his old friend who knew.

"The announcement is on the newspaper's Facebook page. Elle just saw it and she showed me."

"What announcement?" she asked, her heart picking up speed.

"Go online and read it for yourself. I must admit, I'm shocked—I've been reading Aunt Bossy for years and I'd never in my wildest fantasies have suspected she was Quinn. It makes me look at him in quite a different light—he's offered some good advice over the years, and now…"

Bailey didn't hear any more of what her mom had to say. She'd probably get a lecture later for hanging up on her mother, but right now she didn't care.

Less than ten seconds later, her hand was shaking as she held her phone and read Quinn's letter to the world:

A CONFESSION FROM AUNT BOSSY

It has been a privilege and honor to receive your letters over the past years and to offer you what I hoped were words of wisdom. I'm not sure who you thought was answering your letters or if you even cared—I hope that I've helped you solve some of life's dilemmas, but I'm here to tell you that if I have, it was a total fluke.

I am an advice columnist fraud.

For a start, the picture of Aunt Bossy is of an elderly female, whereas I am a twenty-seven-year-old male living in Jewell Rock. I've never been married, divorced or widowed; I've not been in a dispute with my neighbors or sexually harassed by my boss; I haven't even owned a pet; and I'm not a father, although that soon will change. Until recently, I had never even been in love.

Since we're being totally honest, I'll admit that I didn't even believe in love. I thought it was a fairy tale, a nice myth that made movies box-office hits but wasn't at all grounded in reality.

I became Aunt Bossy on a friend's dare, but the truth is I can't even solve my own life issues, so it was a huge audacity to think I could ever hope to fix anyone else's.

My name is Quinn McKinnel and this time I need your help. If you can forgive me for misleading you, and if I have ever offered you any useful advice, I ask that you please consider helping me with my dilemma.

You see, there's this girl who means the world to me—her name's Bailey Sawyer. I've always had the hots for her, even when circumstances meant I really shouldn't. She's without a doubt the best-looking woman on the planet, but she does so much more than turn me on physically. Bailey is warm and kind and funny, she's clever and organized, and it's pure joy to converse with her. She's having my babies, but even if she wasn't, I'd want to be with her. When we're together, I feel more like myself than I ever have before, the world feels as it should be. When we're apart, I think about her constantly and can't wait until I see her again.

But here's what I've learned about love. It can hurt like nothing else and it can make you feel more helpless than anything else ever can. Right now my heart is breaking more than I ever knew it could, because the woman I love, the woman I want to spend the rest of my life with, doesn't believe me.

It's my fault—I've done some stupid, stupid things to her in the past, but I would do anything to be able to take them back, to have a do-over and to be able to prove to Bailey Sawyer that I love her and want to spend the rest of my life making her happy.

By the time she'd finished reading, tears were streaming down Bailey's face. Her phone started ringing again.

"Mom," she answered. "I can't talk right now. Please, give me some time." And then she disconnected and read the letter one more time.

Quinn was going to get a hell of a lot of flak over this letter—she could just imagine the teasing and the jokes that would keep his friends and family in hysterics for some time. Blair and Mac especially would dine out on this for the rest of their days. But even more than that, now that this confession was out in the public sphere, he'd probably have to give up his role as Aunt Bossy—a role that he was strangely good at, and one that she now knew he enjoyed.

What on earth had possessed him to do such a thing?

Somewhere in the back of her head a little voice piped up. *Love, Bailey. He did it because he loves you.*

Confused, she flopped back against the pillows and

thought back to last night when he'd told her he wouldn't have sex with her unless she believed in them like he did.

Her heart jolted as realization struck.

He hadn't said *have sex*, he'd said *make love*!

He'd said *make love* instead of *sleep together* or *have sex* or that other coarse word he could have used to describe what she'd been offering. Bailey closed her eyes as she remembered the reverent tone he'd used and the hurt she'd seen in his eyes. She'd been too shocked, too angry and humiliated, to take notice of his pain, but she could suddenly see it for what it was.

Absolutely raw, painfully real.

He'd been standing before her in that same gorgeous body he'd always had, but there'd been something different about him. He was no longer trying to charm the pants off her. Instead, he was opening up and telling her how he felt.

And she'd thrown it all back in his face.

She clutched her phone with Quinn's confession against her chest. Could she dare to believe that he truly did love her? Could she dare to believe he would love her even if she wasn't pregnant with his babies? She'd burned his jacket, she'd purposely forgotten to tell him about an ultrasound and then found out the babies' sexes without him being there, she'd avoided him like he was an infectious disease, yet he'd still tried to connect with her, still sent her daily messages to check on her and still said he wanted her.

He wanted her so much that he wouldn't take advantage of her emotions and sleep with her. And he wouldn't let her take advantage of him. She knew then that if he didn't love her, he *would* have slept with her. He'd have been more than happy to oblige.

"Oh, God, what have I done?"

Quinn loved her and she loved him, more than she'd ever dreamed possible. No one had ever made her feel with the intensity that he did—anger, happiness, sadness, *love*. With him, everything was amplified.

In holding on to the past—to the mistakes that had got them where they were today, in refusing to forgive him for not immediately coming clean about the letter, in not trusting or believing that he loved her, had she been cutting off her nose to spite her face?

She scrambled out of bed and into the shower. She needed to see Quinn ASAP, but first she needed to find the perfect leather jacket.

"Hi, Uncle Quinn." The moment Quinn stepped into his mom's house late Saturday afternoon, his niece Hallie launched herself at him and threw her arms around his middle.

"Hey, princess," he said, welcoming the hug from his niece. He loved his niece and nephew with all his heart and they loved him back in the uncomplicated way that only children could. It was a pity all relationships weren't so effortless. Not in the mood for a party—even one that would involve all his favorite junk food from when he was a kid—he forced a smile and handed Hallie one of the two gifts he'd brought with him. "Happy Birthday."

Grinning up at him with her big blue eyes, she took the gift. "Thank you." And then she nodded toward the other present. "Is that one for Hamish?"

"Sure is. Where is he?"

"He's in the family room playing with the train set Granny Nora gave him. Where's Bailey?"

Quinn swallowed. The last time he'd seen his niece

had been at his mom's birthday party and he guessed no one had mentioned to Hallie that he and Bailey were no longer an item. "She's not feeling that great."

Before Hallie could respond to that, Blair sauntered down the hallway toward them. He took one look at Quinn and broke out into hysterical laughter. Clutching his stomach, he called over his shoulder toward the kitchen, where Quinn guessed the rest of his family were congregated. "Hey, everyone! Aunt Bossy is here. Everyone got your questions ready?"

"Ha-ha," Quinn said, bracing himself as he followed Blair into the kitchen, which was decorated in balloons and streamers for the twins' family party.

He'd already spoken to his mom and sisters this morning, but that didn't stop them smirking a little. Since his confession had appeared on the newspaper's Facebook page late last night, it felt like he'd heard from every person living in Jewell Rock, but the one person he'd wanted to touch with his words had been conspicuously silent. He'd been getting emails and messages all morning from women—not offering advice as he'd requested, but offering themselves on platters instead. He'd have switched off his phone and crawled into a hole if not for the possibility Bailey might try to get in contact with him. All day he'd been holding out hope that she would, but now, as it headed toward nightfall, that hope was dwindling fast.

Lachlan held up the local newspaper and started reading from a recent Aunt Bossy column, putting on a high-pitched, whiny voice. "Dear Aunt Bossy, I've been married for fifteen years, but I secretly still lust after my high school sweetheart. I recently looked him up on Facebook…"

"So what did you get for your birthday, Hallie?" Quinn

asked, speaking over the top of his brother as he pulled out a seat and sat at the table.

"Did you even have a high school sweetheart?" Blair asked, not giving Hallie the chance to answer.

Sophie sat down beside Quinn and elbowed him. "Is this for real? Are you seriously Aunt Bossy?"

"What do you know about fixing other people's problems?" Callum asked with a chuckle.

Quinn reached out and grabbed a glass, his fingers curling around it as he poured himself a drink from a bottle of cola on the table. Was it too early to add a measure of whiskey? If it weren't for not wanting to upset Hallie and Hamish, he'd never have left the house today. Right now he had enough self-loathing that he didn't need to take more crap from his brothers and sisters.

"You know what?" he snapped, glancing from one of his siblings to the next. "Perhaps I know more than any of you have ever given me credit for."

And then he let loose. He zeroed in on Mac first. "I know you messed up big-time in your career, but you're not the first soccer player to kick an own goal and you sure won't be the last. Either stop feeling sorry for yourself and go back to the game, or move on and stop being such a grump. There's more to life than winning."

Mac raised his eyebrows and took a sip of his drink, but Quinn continued. He looked to Callum. "Make sure you don't screw things up with Chelsea, because she's way better than you deserve and sometimes you don't know how good you've got something until it's gone. And, Annabel, I know you loved Blake and that you feel like you'll never find anyone else that matches up to him, but you need to move on, or you may as well have died, too.

"Blair and Claire." He looked to where they sat next to each other across the table. "I don't know if you guys noticed, but you got a divorce—it's time someone told you that the whole concept of getting divorced means actually separating your lives. From where I'm sitting, you look more like newlyweds than divorcees. If breaking up was a mistake, then get the hell back together, but if not, it's time to cut loose and move on."

He was on a roll, but he took a quick sip of his drink before turning to Sophie. "And, you." He pointed his finger at her. "What's with this lesbian joke? If you don't want Mom to hassle you about dating, then tell her, don't make up some stupid story about liking pussy."

His mom, who'd been standing by the oven, gasped and covered her mouth. Quinn wasn't sure if she was shocked by his words or by the fact that Sophie had been having her on.

"But while we're on the subject of dating," he continued." What are you so afraid of, Soph?"

She blinked, opened her mouth and then closed it again, so Quinn directed his finger at Lachlan. "I've got stuff for you, too." He glanced at Hallie, who'd been watching the conversation earnestly. "But I'll tell you later."

His family sat around the table in stunned silence for a few moments, and Quinn waited to feel better for getting all this off his chest, but it didn't happen. Instead, he felt like a jerk for having such an outburst when they were supposed to be celebrating Hamish and Hallie's birthday. He realized he was giving Mac a run for his money for the title of Family Grump.

Finally, Nora spoke. "Well, now that we've got that out of the way, shall we have lunch?" Good old Mom—her answer to everything was always food and he'd be sure to apologize for his behavior later. Even if he ardently believed everything he'd told his brothers and sisters, this dinner hadn't been the time to tell them.

Everyone jumped on this bandwagon, leaping up from their various chairs to help Mom carry the homemade pizzas, garlic bread and token salad to the table. As usual, there was enough food to feed an army and for a moment he thought about packaging up some leftovers and taking them over to Bailey. It was now more important than ever that she eat well.

But he quickly discarded this idea—she'd made it clear she didn't want anything more than his body.

Once the food was all laid out, everyone resumed their seats. Hamish was called in from the family room and, blissfully oblivious to the tension in the room, he chattered away, telling everyone about the track he'd just built. Conversation turned to other things, but Quinn didn't even attempt to participate. He vaguely registered Annabel telling everyone about a suspicious fire she'd attended last week and Callum talking about an idea he'd had for a whiskey club, but truthfully he was lost in his own hopeless thoughts.

Perhaps it would be better if he just left. He felt bad for his niece and nephew, but he was in no mood to celebrate. He was about to stand up when the doorbell jingled its chirpy tune.

"I'll get it," Sophie said. She pushed back her seat and headed toward the front door. Quinn guessed it might be another one of the "friends" she'd been parading in front of Mom lately to encourage the suspicion that she was a lesbian. Normally he'd enjoy the joke, but he found very little funny right at the moment.

He picked up a piece of pizza and took a mammoth bite, then almost choked as Bailey appeared in the doorway.

Sophie look pleased with herself. "Look who I found."

"Hi, everyone." Bailey lifted a hand to wave and her eyes came to rest on him. His gut felt hollow despite all the food he'd just devoured.

He swallowed, unable to speak as his family took their turns greeting the mother of his babies. It was then he noticed that she held a black leather jacket in her other hand.

"Do you want to sit down?" Annabel said. "Quinn told me about the twin-to-twin transfusion thing. I'm really sorry."

Bailey nodded and then cleared her throat. "Actually, I need to talk to Quinn."

"Would you two like some privacy?" Nora asked. "You won't be disturbed in the family room."

Bailey shook her head. "No, it's okay. I want to say this in front of everyone who matters to Quinn." Then she held up the jacket and looked straight at him. "I got this for you. I know it's not exactly the same as your old one and I'm so sorry for ruining that one, but I hope you like it."

"Cool!" exclaimed Hamish as Bailey stepped toward Quinn and proffered the jacket.

He found himself turning in his chair to face her, then he reached out and took it.

"Try it on," she said, with a nod of encouragement.

Not sure what to say or think, he did as she said, threading his arms into the jacket. He had to admit it fit almost perfectly, and in spite of the smell of new leather, it was almost as soft as his old one had been after years of wear and tear.

"It looks great. Do you like it?" Bailey asked.

"I like it fine." Quinn raised an eyebrow, expecting a reprimand for rudeness from his mom, but everyone was watching them and no one was saying a word.

She smiled. "I'm glad."

Was that it? She came over here to give him a leather jacket? Whether he liked the jacket or not didn't matter. If he couldn't have her, he didn't want anything *from* her. Clothing included. "Is that the only reason you came? To give me a new jacket?"

She rubbed her lips one over the other as she often did when she was nervous.

"Well, that's not the only reason," she admitted and then dropped to her knees in front of him.

Quinn felt his eyes boggle in his head and he instinctively reached out to steady her. She may only be five months pregnant, but she was already almost as big as some women were at full-term. She had no business being on the floor. "Get up off there!"

Bailey shook her head, held up her hand and gazed up at him, her beautiful forest green eyes glistening with water. "Quinn McKinnel, I *believe* you." It took him a second to register those three words.

"You do?" he whispered.

She nodded and reached up to hold his hands. "I saw your confession and I'm sorry you had to go that far to prove your love to me. You are the father of my babies, and because of that you'll always be special to me, but it's much more than that. You are also my friend and the man I love with all my heart. I'm sorry I didn't believe in your love at first—I was scared, but I hope in time you'll forgive me and I hope you'll also do me the great honor of becoming my husband."

"Are you for real?" Quinn had never been more

shocked in his life. Had Bailey just proposed to him? She wanted *him* to forgive *her*?

But even as he asked these questions, he knew that marriage was not something Bailey took lightly or would ever joke about. He tried to swallow as a ball of emotion erupted in the back of his throat. His eyes took their turn to water, and gazing down at her, he knew he was in very real danger of crying like a girl in front of his brothers. He didn't care. At least his tears would give them something new to rib him about aside from Aunt Bossy. And if this wasn't some cruel joke or torturous dream, any teasing would be more than worth it.

"Yes, sure am. I know we've done everything backward and in a nontraditional way," Bailey continued, her voice a little shaky, "so I hope you'll forgive me for breaking tradition one more time and asking *you* to marry *me*, but I wanted to show you that I do believe in you and your love. I love you back and I want nothing more than to be your wife. What do you say?"

In reply, Quinn leaned over in his seat and captured her face in his hands. He brushed his thumbs over her smooth cheeks as he leaned forward and kissed her on the lips. Marriage, the thing he'd always vowed to stay clear of, suddenly felt like the biggest prize of his life.

"That's a yes, in case you were wondering," he said as he came up for air. "And I'm a feminist, so I'm more than happy for you to do the proposing honors. I'll even take your surname if that's what you want."

As long as they were together, he didn't give two hoots about the little things.

She laughed and a tear sneaked from the corner of her right eye and rolled down her cheek. "Now, let's not get too carried away. As you said, Bailey McKinnel has a nice ring to it."

All around them his family burst into shrieks and cheers of congratulations, but Quinn barely registered the excitement. He couldn't look away from Bailey.

"I do love you," he whispered, brushing another runaway tear off her cheek with his thumb.

"I know you do," she whispered back. And he could see the truth in her eyes. "I would have come quicker, but I've spent all day looking for the perfect engagement jacket."

He chuckled. "Does this mean I don't have to buy you a ring?"

"No way!" She held up her hand and wriggled her fingers at him. "I want a big one!"

Everyone laughed.

"I think this calls for a toast," Nora said, clapping her hands to get her family's attention. "But since there are two pregnant women at the table, it will have to be orange juice all round!"

"Oh, dear," Bailey said as she tried to get up from her position on the floor. "Maybe it was a little silly to get down so low in my current predicament."

"Yeah. Don't do it again, alright?" Smiling down at her, Quinn offered his hands and helped her off the floor.

"Can we have the cake now?" Hamish asked.

"Yeah," Hallie said with a slight moan. "It's our birthday, remember?"

Everyone laughed and Quinn helped Bailey into a seat at the table. Dragging his own chair closer, he wrapped his arm around her and drew her into his side. Now that he had her back again, he never wanted to let her go.

He wasn't naive enough to think that things would be

smooth sailing from here on in—they still had the appointment with the TTTS specialist and the rest of Bailey's pregnancy to get through—but whatever life threw at them next, they would deal with it together. With this knowledge, he pressed his lips against her cheek—a chaste kiss with the promise of much more to come later—and whispered, "Welcome to the family, sweetheart."

Epilogue

AUNT BOSSY TIES THE KNOT

Regular readers of our popular Aunt Bossy (aka Quinn Robert McKinnel) column will be interested to know that our beloved advice columnist has tied the knot.

Quinn, son of Conall (dec.) and Nora McKinnel of Jewell Rock, and Bailey Ann Sawyer, daughter of Marcia and Reginald Wallace, also of Jewell Rock, were married last Saturday on the grounds of McKinnel's Distillery.

The ceremony was performed by the bride's stepfather, Reginald, in front of the distillery's beautiful lake and was attended by a crowd of well-wishers from their hometown. The bride, dressed in a stunning gown designed by local Cindy Lemmon, was attended by the grooms' twin sisters, Annabel and Sophie, and her own younger sister, Elle.

The groom, with his four brothers as grooms-men, embraced his family's Scottish heritage by wearing the McKinnel tartan. Blair McKinnel played the bridal march on his bagpipes.

But it was the couple's six-month-old twin sons, Avery and Morgan, dressed in kilts to match their father's and carried down the aisle by their grand-mothers, who stole the show.

The romantic reception that followed in the distillery's newly opened restaurant was for close friends and family only. Credit must go to the blushing bride for organizing the event—as if giving birth to gorgeous twin boys wasn't enough to keep her busy, Bailey has also taken on the role of Director of Events at McKinnel's Distillery and is already gaining a strong reputation for organizing the most magical events in Jewell Rock.

The couple's wedding was the fifth held at the distillery since the new restaurant opened last summer, with the first also being a family wedding between the groom's older brother Callum and his new wife, Chelsea, who attended Quinn and Bailey's wedding with their three-month-old daughter, Nora Jean.

The grand reception feast was catered by the groom's brother, and the restaurant's head chef, Lachlan McKinnel, and his fiancée, Eliza, who also works at the distillery restaurant.

The happy couple have chosen to delay their honeymoon until their boys are older but are looking forward to moving into their new family home, currently under construction supervised by another of the groom's brothers, Owen (Mac) McKinnel.

Turn to page 35 for Aunt Bossy's latest advice offering.

* * * * *

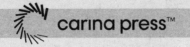
Ben handed Laney a sealed envelope, then walked around the back of the partial chair. "Quite a project you've got here."

"I probably should have taken a nap after the first one." She peeled the flap off the envelope and pulled out a folded paper.

Inside was a short, handwritten note. *I think you should go for it.*

All of a sudden, her cheeks felt warm and she wanted to hide the words against her chest or crumple the paper so there was no chance Ben could read it, even though he'd probably have no idea what her cousin meant by it. Instead she refolded the paper and slid it back into the envelope. Then she pressed the flap down the best she could before lifting the toolbox and sliding it underneath.

"Everything okay?" he asked.

"Yeah." She looked up at him, her mind flailing for some reasonable explanation why Nola would ask Ben to deliver something to her. "Just some information I needed about getting a Maine driver's license and plates for my car and… stuff."

Please don't ask me why she didn't just call or text the information, she thought as soon as the words left her mouth.

"Cool. Do you need some help with this chair?"

"No, thank you. I've got it."

"Want some company?"

"Sure." She wondered if he'd make it five minutes before he leaned in and tried to tighten a bolt for her before just building the rest of it himself. "Want a drink?"

He held up an insulated tumbler as he sat in her folding camp chair, shaking it so the ice rattled. "I have one, thanks. Do you need a fresh one?"

Laney kept her face down, looking at the instruction sheet, so he wouldn't see her smile. He was so polite, but she didn't want to imagine him in her camper. He wasn't as tall as Josh, but he had broad shoulders and she could picture him filling the space. If they were both in there, they'd brush against each other trying to get by…and her imagination needed to change the subject before she started blushing again.

"No, thanks," she said. "I'm good."

"Okay. Yesterday's accident aside, how are you liking the Northern Star? And Whitford in general, I guess."

"I haven't seen too much of Whitford yet. The market and gas station, and the hardware store. And obviously I'll be going to the town hall soon."

"You haven't eaten at the Trailside Diner yet?"

"No, but Nola brought me a sandwich from there yesterday. Right before the accident. It was really good."

"Their dinner menu is even better."

Was he working his way around to asking her out to dinner? It had been so long since she'd dated, she wasn't sure if she was reading too much into a friendly conversation. But it seemed her next line would naturally be *I'll have to try it sometime* and then he'd say *How about tomorrow night?* or something like that.

And she had no idea how she felt about that.

Don't miss
WHAT IT TAKES:
A KOWALSKI REUNION NOVEL
by Shannon Stacey, available wherever books are sold.

www.CarinaPress.com